CRANFORD PUBLIC LIBRARY NJ

3 9520 00268 1718

AUG 5 2011

P9-CLG-387

B+T

DEATH IN
HIGH PLACES

Also by Jo Bannister

DEATH IN
HIGH PLACES

JO BANNISTER

MINOTAUR BOOKS ⚏ NEW YORK

This is a work of fiction. All of the characters, organizations, and events portrayed in this novel are either products of the author's imagination or are used fictitiously.

DEATH IN HIGH PLACES. Copyright © 2011 by Jo Bannister. All rights reserved. Printed in the United States of America. For information, address St. Martin's Press, 175 Fifth Avenue, New York, N.Y. 10010.

www.minotaurbooks.com

Library of Congress Cataloging-in-Publication Data

Bannister, Jo.
   Death in high places / Jo Bannister.—1st ed.
      p. cm.
   Summary: "Two friends embark on a climb of treacherous Anarchy Ridge but only one will make it down alive. Unjustly blamed for his friend's haunting death, the other must run for his life as a mourning father seeks revenge"—Provided by publisher.
   ISBN 978-0-312-57353-9
   1. Mountaineering accidents—Fiction. 2. Fathers—Fiction. 3. Revenge—Fiction. 4. Assassins—Fiction. I. Title.
   PR6052.A497D43 2011
   823'.91—dc22

2011009109

First Edition: August 2011

10 9 8 7 6 5 4 3 2 1

PROLOGUE

THE FIRST THING YOU NEED TO KNOW about mountains is that they don't care. They're not out to get you, nor have they any interest in keeping you alive. They are supremely indifferent to the presence of tiny humans among their crags and pinnacles. Every time you go to the mountains, you have to remember that they don't care whether you come back.

People who spend a lot of time at sea say that sometimes—not always, not reliably, but sometimes—the sea seems to enjoy having you there. Provides for your comfort, tries to keep you safe. No one feels that way about mountains. They're cold. And not just those jutting their heads into the region of perennial snows known as the Death Zone. There are desert mountains whose red rocks become too hot to touch under the unblinking sun, but at the heart of them even they are cold.

On the bright side, they're not actually trying to kill you. But their very nature is hugely inimical to human survival. They don't have to do anything to get you killed. Just being a mountain is often enough.

Which is precisely why young men climb. They embrace the challenge. They want to test themselves, test their manhood, in one of the few environments where the Health & Safety Inspectorate doesn't get a look-in. The first time they approach a real killer mountain they're like any other virgin, innocent, unprepared. Whatever they may tell their friends, they may be afraid every minute they're up there. But even fear can be addictive. If you genuinely think you're going to die, and then you don't, the flood of euphoria is better than anything you can buy on a Friday night from men in hoodies. That's what keeps you going back. You tell people you're hooked on climbing. Actually, you're hooked on coming back down.

The second thing you need to know about mountains is that a significant proportion of those who get to the top—who stand in triumph on the highest point of their chosen peak while their companions take bad photographs with chilled hands clumsy in big gloves—never see base camp again.

Consider these two. They're in their early twenties, as fit and strong as it's possible for human beings to be. They have all the right gear. One of them, the taller, has brand-new high-tech clothing and kit in this year's fashion color, which happens to be lime green. The other is wearing last year's outfit and carrying a combination of sound old gear and newer stuff bought secondhand from climbers who care what color's in fashion. None of it matches. All of it is good quality and well maintained.

People who saw them setting out, days ago and many miles away across the trackless foothills, assumed that he was the guide and the taller man in the Day-Glo green was the client. In fact they were mistaken about that. They're both amateurs, in the truest sense of the word, young men who've crossed first an ocean and then a continent to reach their chosen mountain, to pit themselves against an untried peak in one of the few parts of the world where you can still find such a thing—Alaska. The only reason for the difference in their appearance is that one has more money than the other.

Right now they're running on anticipation. Their bodies are tired—they've carried their kit a long way over broken terrain, and they'll carry it a good deal farther before they can finally start the climb proper—but their minds are buzzing with excitement. An expedition like this doesn't come together in a bar on a Saturday night. They've been planning it for two years. They've done plenty of climbs together in that time, at home in Britain, in the European Alps, in the High Atlas of North Africa. But Alaska has always been the goal, and almost since they started their research this mountain has been the one they wanted. Mostly because there's no record of its having been climbed before. It's not as high as Mount McKinley. It's probably not the hardest climb in the state. But it's a chance to set their boots on slopes that may never have felt them before, and the romance of that captivates them. They'll deny it to their dying day, but all climbers are romantics.

They've seen pictures. Aerial photographs of the summit, and pictures taken by earlier expeditions of the approaches and also the main obstacle to success, an exposed ridge two-thirds of the way up where the wind has honed the rock to a knife-edge under a coating of green ice. The mountain has a name, though it's not a very impressive one—it's called Little Horse, and the river winding round its feet is the Little Horse River. Oddly enough, the ridge is more famous. It's the highest point known to have been reached by earlier climbers, none of whom found a way across. Some of those who attempted it turned back, some died. Those who turned back named the ridge, and the name they gave it tells you all you need to know about the conditions they found there. They called it Anarchy Ridge.

Our two young men are still a long way short of Anarchy Ridge. They haven't even crossed the Little Horse River yet, and after that they have to climb up onto the glacier that inches down the shoulder of the mountain, grinding its unseen rocks to gravel. They won't set up base camp until late tomorrow. It's as well that the thrill of anticipation is keeping them going. There isn't much else here to enjoy.

Except one another's company. Once the climb starts in earnest, there won't be time to talk—just a terse trading of advice, warnings and swear words until either they succeed or are beaten back. There'll be time in the tent at night, but by then they won't have any energy left for conversation. Only if the weather keeps them pinned down will they have both the time and the inclination to socialize.

But now, with all the danger and excitement and challenge still ahead of them, whatever breath the broken ground doesn't demand of them can be spared for talking. Being young men, their conversation isn't particularly profound. It revolves around women, and work, and how many pints you can sink before you get that funny tunnel-vision effect, and soccer, and fast cars. The tall one can afford a fast car. The short one can afford a car. Because they're friends, the short one mocks the tall one for being rich; the tall one does not mock the short one for being comparatively poor. Both are absolutely comfortable with this and show it by the easy nature of their insults.

"Then there was the one with buck teeth," says the short one. "I mean, what kind of a combination is that—an open-topped car and a girlfriend with buck teeth? Did you polish the flies off them before you kissed her good night?"

"Louise did *not* have buck teeth," says the tall one, with dignity and the lilt of an Irish accent. "She had what my mother described as a patrician profile. Also, she had nice manners. She polished the flies off herself."

"Patrick, your mother could find the silver lining in a week full of wet Wednesdays! Why else . . . ?" He stops himself just in time. There are some insults that even really good friends shouldn't trade.

Tall Patrick hears what hasn't been said and laughs it off with a lightness that falls just short of convincing. "Would she marry my father? Because she knew what a devastatingly handsome son he'd give her, of course!"

The other one scowls into the wind, ruing his gauche attempt at humor and admiring Patrick's deftness in deflecting it. He didn't mean to hurt his friend but he knows he has, and also that Patrick will neither hold the grudge nor turn it back. He doesn't envy his companion the family money that funds his share of their expeditions. He certainly doesn't envy Patrick his family. But he does sometimes, in the privacy of his own head where no one will ever suspect, envy him his education. Not because he has a use for Latin verbs, but because he thinks a better education would have equipped him to deal more graciously with the world, the way Patrick does. He doesn't underestimate his own strengths, as a climber and as a man—his compact, hardy physique, his endless endurance, and the mental toughness that, indistinguishable from obstinacy, keeps him going long after any reasonable person would have quit. But he wishes there was more about him to like. Everyone likes Patrick. With Patrick, there's nothing *not* to like.

He steers the conversation back onto safer ground. "Then there's the one with pigtails. You know, the one who took up climbing so the two of you would have something in common. Who'd have taken up sheep-shearing or necrophilia if she'd thought it was something you could do together."

But Patrick doesn't laugh, and when his friend glances back he catches a thoughtful expression on Patrick's face. "Don't poke fun at her. That's a seriously nice girl, and I'm damned if I know what to do about her."

The shorter man shrugs. "Have her, make her breakfast, and begin your next sentence with the words, 'It's not you, it's me' . . ."

Patrick arches a disapproving eyebrow. "Nicky, I have never in my life dumped a girl like that, and I'm not starting with her. What's more, I don't think you would either. You're full of it, you know that? You talk like Jack the lad, but if it came right down to it—if first of all you could *find* someone who wanted to be your girl-friend, and then she wanted to stick with you after you wanted to move on—I think you'd emigrate and send her a postcard from Brisbane. Wouldn't you? I've seen you talking to women, remember. If they don't know a piton from a crampon, you have no bloody idea what to say to them."

Which is true. It's something else Nicky rather regrets. He just thinks there'll be time to worry about it later. After he's climbed all the mountains he wants to. "All right then, marry her. Have kids and a Volvo estate with her."

"I can't do that either. It wouldn't be fair."

"It's what she wants. Anyone who's seen her looking at you knows that."

"I know it too. Nicky, none of this is news to me. But it wouldn't be right. I like her. I like her a lot. I don't like her enough. And she doesn't need to be my second choice, or anybody else's. She deserves better than that."

"Hold on." Nicky stops and looks his friend squarely in the face. "Is this your way of telling me there's someone else? Someone you *do* like enough?"

Even elegant, well-bred Patrick looks discomfited. "Maybe. I don't know."

"Well, who is she?"

But Patrick knows better than to answer. "And have it the subject of common gossip in every bothy from the Pamirs to the Rockies? I don't think so!"

Nicky shrugs, untroubled. "So don't tell me. But if that's the problem, maybe you should tell"—he still can't remember her name—"her with the pigtails."

Patrick looks serious again. "I know. I'm just wondering how. I don't want to hurt her."

"You're *going* to hurt her," says Nicky, relationship expert. "And sooner is better than later."

"I know," says Patrick sadly.

After they've crossed the Little Horse River and they're standing at the foot of the glacier, looking up, they still can't see the summit of the mountain, only its heaving shoulders. But they can see the thin blade of the ridge, and the snow whipped off it by the rising wind making arabesques against the impossibly blue sky. They stand still for a long time, their kit at their feet, just looking.

Finally Patrick says, "And we're going up there, are we?"

Nicky grins his youthful, overconfident grin and nods. "Oh yeah."

"All the way?"

"You'd better believe it."

But there's a word for people who put their trust in mountains. You see it sometimes inscribed on memorials. Not even tombstones: you make that big a mistake, it's unlikely they'll find enough of you to bury.

The mountain waits. The weather closes in. The blue sky vanishes under the swirling gray cloak of a spring storm. Snow falls, and also rises as the wind tears it off the mountain's sides. There are no observers, but if there were there would be nothing to observe. In a whiteout, you can die of exposure scant meters from the shelter that you cannot find. If there had been any observers, they would not have believed it possible that anyone could survive, let alone climb, in that.

But there is only the mountain. And when eventually the whiteout subsides and the sky turns blue again, and the expedition trudges exhaustedly down from the Death Zone and out onto the last treacherous traverse across the glacier, Little Horse doesn't even notice that the climbing party is smaller coming down than it was when it went up.

CHAPTER I

HE'D GOT IN THE WAY of returning home at different times and by different routes. The first thing he did when he moved to a new town was rehearse the alternatives, driving and on foot, and make a note of where it was normal to see parked cars and men standing on street corners and where it wasn't. After four years it was second nature to him.

After four years the whole business had become second nature. Finding work where he could get cash in hand and no one would want his National Insurance number. Finding somewhere to live where paying the rent in advance would save him having to prove who he was. His name was Nicky Horn. But that wasn't the name the world knew him by. It wasn't even one of them.

All the lies he told—the mislaid driver's license, the stolen passport, the pink slip that got lost in the post—would never have stood up to serious scrutiny. But they never had to. Before anyone got sufficiently interested to start checking him out he'd packed his bag, thrown his tools in the back of the car and moved on. He'd been doing it for nearly as long as he'd been back in England. It worked pretty well on the whole. It was months since he'd felt death breathing on the back of his neck.

And that was a problem too. The better he got at this, the more distance he put between himself and pursuit, the greater the risk of complacency. Complacency can be the biggest killer of all. Bigger than hatred, bigger than love. As perilous as sunshine on snow. He was stronger, fitter and faster than his pursuers, and he wanted to live even more than they wanted him dead. The biggest danger was not that they'd wear him down, although one day they might; or that they might get lucky, though that too was always a possibility. The biggest danger was that one day he might dare to think he was safe. To relax and let down his guard. He'd never be safe. He knew that now. If he ever allowed himself to entertain the idea, even for a moment, even as a daydream, he might as well cut his own throat. Cut his own rope. It would be a cleaner end, and no more certain.

The other thing was, he was getting tired. Physically tired—the constant moving, the broken nights, the fact that even when he slept he did so with one ear cocked, might be considered a natural part of a young man's life, but they took their toll when extended over four years—but also mentally and emotionally. The things he'd done, the lies he'd told. He was sick and tired of the whole sorry business. Sometimes in the long hard watches of the night he thought it might be better to stop running, to let events take their course. He wasn't afraid of dying. He'd never been afraid of dying. But he used to have more to live for.

He gave himself a shake. He couldn't afford to think like that. You don't give up; you never give up. There's always a way down the mountain—you just have to find it. Tommy Hanratty wasn't a young man. He could die. And he wasn't a good man—someone could kill him. Horn knew it was a long shot. But when it's the only kind you're likely to get, you take the long shot and hope for the best.

Sometimes that was the hardest part of all. Keeping hope alive.

Despite the spring rain he left his car a street away and walked the last hundred yards. He wasn't sure but he thought it was a good idea. If he found himself cornered one day, Hanratty's hirelings would find it harder to predict his actions if they weren't sure where his car was. He could sneak out the back way and circle round with some confidence that they'd be watching the house where he was lodging, not the next street. The people where he lived didn't even know he had a car. Sometimes he made sure they saw him using the bus. Psychologists call it compartmentalization. You build barriers between the different parts of your life, in the hope that when the shit hits the fan there'll always be somewhere clean where you can hide.

Nicky Horn believed he'd become an expert in compartmentalization. In fact he was wrong about that. The shit had hit the fan before he knew he needed barriers, and the smell tainted every aspect of his life. He'd just got used to it.

A couple of cars he didn't recognize were parked on the corner. Probably it meant nothing. Since he got here two months ago someone had opened a sandwich bar. Which was handy for a man whose idea of cooking was to reheat a pot of coffee, but it made it harder to spot the faces that didn't fit, the strangers with no obvious business in the area. He'd learned it was safer not to take a room opposite a factory or a pub, but things change. Someone opened a sandwich bar the week before last, and it was time he moved on.

There was a man in one of the cars. The light from the streetlamps bouncing off the wet road was enough to show a face that would have been unreadable on a better night. Still mostly from habit Horn gave him a glance as he walked past—casual enough not to arouse curiosity, long enough to remember what he saw. A middle-aged man in a dark coat. Narrow, longish face, no glasses or mustache, short graying hair. Hard to say how tall when he was sitting down. He looked up as Horn looked down and their eyes met for a second, then the man looked away—unhurriedly, checking the mirror. Waiting for someone in the café, probably. Horn walked on, his toolbag slung over his shoulder, crossed the road and went home.

It was gone ten o'clock. He took overtime when he could get it, to make up for the times when he'd had to leave a good job without collecting his pay because the look on a stranger's face said he'd been recognized. More than once, he was sure, he'd read too much into an everyday exchange of glances and fled his latest job and his latest bed because someone had nothing better to do than idly watch the passersby. It couldn't be helped. He had to act on instinct. If he waited for proof it would be too late.

And then, he thought his face was more famous than it was. Because he remembered what happened as if it were yesterday, he thought everyone else did too.

There was a grainy television in his room but he didn't turn it on. He watched when there was something to watch, but background noise was never a good idea. He needed to hear the unexpected footstep, the soft hand trying the door. He dropped his tools in a corner, hung his jacket on the nail, eased his feet out of his boots and lay down on top of the bed with his eyes closed. It was a comfortable bed, the best he'd had for more than a year. He'd miss it when he left.

The sharp silhouettes of mountains appeared on the inside of his eyelids. But he couldn't afford the distraction of a flashback. He sat up abruptly, reached out and turned on the TV. There was nothing worth watching, but anything was better than the memories. Tonight he'd take the risk of numbing his senses.

Talking heads came on the screen. Horn tried to concentrate, but it was politics or economics or international trade, one of those subjects that he knew affected him but failed to engage his interest. Slumped on his comfortable bed, bone tired, lulled by knowledgeable voices using words he didn't understand when he was awake, still fully dressed he slid sideways into sleep.

Sometime later—he couldn't judge how long: the economists on the TV had given way to a cartoon dog with subtitles but nothing else appeared to have changed—something woke him. He sat up with a guilty start, as if he were being paid to stay awake. While his senses were still working out where in his brain they belonged, his well-trained body had already moved into self-preservation mode, rolling silently off the bed, padding sock-footed into the corner beside the door and away from the window.

He wished he'd turned the TV off earlier. He couldn't do it now without advertising the fact that he was awake. He sipped shallow breaths and listened with all his being.

He heard nothing. With his ear against the door he still heard nothing. He reached down carefully and slipped the special hammer out of its pocket in his bag. Successive colleagues laughed when he said it was a present from a girlfriend and he wanted to keep it nice, and anyway it was a lie. The point of the thick sock he kept wrapped around its head was that he didn't want to be responsible for another death.

The fingers of his left hand rested butterfly-light on the door handle. Half a second before it turned he'd feel if someone grasped the other side. He felt nothing. He went on waiting, and still nothing happened, nothing changed. Which left him with a choice: to open the door and look, to go back to bed, or to sit up all night in the fireside chair with his hammer on his lap, waiting for someone to storm in here. Aware that what disturbed him just might have been the old lady from downstairs looking for her cat, he held the hammer behind him and opened the door with his left hand.

A weak yellow light burned on the landing all night. There was no furniture to cast shadows or conceal an intruder, just the stairs that went up and the stairs that went down. No one was there. A couple of swift steps took him to the stairwell and he looked up and down, and still he saw no one.

He emptied his lungs in a soft, ragged sigh and drew a proper breath for the first time in five minutes. A false alarm. Another one.

He didn't have a clock. He put the hammer down on the bed, parted the curtains and angled his watch to the streetlamp outside. A little before three o'clock. The sandwich bar had closed and no one was on the street. Finally he turned off the TV.

But he'd forgotten something. Something so basic it took him a moment to remember what it was. He'd listened at the door, he'd checked the landing, up the stairs and down, come back inside, checked the time . . .

He hadn't locked the door behind him.

Even as he reached for it, it opened and there was a man in the room with him. As quickly as that. He must have taken at least a couple of steps but Horn didn't see them. Lacking only the puff of smoke, he arrived like the evil magician on a pantomime stage—not there one second, there the next. The room was still dark—darker, now, without the television—so Horn couldn't see the face, only the silhouette against the weak light from the landing. Even so, he knew two things about him. This wasn't one of Hanratty's in-house heavies, he was too good. And although Horn couldn't see it, he had a gun in his hand. Not in a pocket, not under his arm—in his hand, ready for immediate use. Eighteen months ago the old thug had grown tired of failure, put the contract out to tender and started employing professionals.

Horn had run out of luck at last. Being strong, fit and fast isn't enough against a professional killer. A bullet traveling at twice the speed of sound is always going to be faster.

"Nicholas Horn?" The voice told him nothing. No regional accent, no indication of age, no patois of class—all the tags that might help identify him had been rigorously schooled out of it. Early in his career this man had spent hours talking to a tape recorder and playing it back, listening acutely and analyzing what he heard; and he hadn't felt even slightly foolish doing it. A pro. A genuine, twenty-four-karat, blink-and-you'll-miss-him hit man.

Horn had got a bit of a shock the first time he realized the all-purpose muscle Hanratty used to police his narcotics empire and operate his protection rackets had been superseded by someone with real skill and finesse. Someone expert, and expensive. Hanratty had decided that nothing mattered to him—not the Bentley, not the yacht, not the family acres in Ireland or the house in Bloomsbury or the contents of all those numbered bank accounts, *nothing*—so much as repaying the man who killed his son. Though a combination of good luck and good reactions allowed him to escape even as the net closed, Horn knew he'd never be as lucky again. That now he had a pro on his case, he was as good as dead. That this moment would come, when he was face-to-face with the man who'd taken Hanratty's contract, and this time running would not be an option.

Only basic survival instinct, the absolute determination of living things to keep living as long as possible, kept him from making a bad mistake. He was not entirely unarmed. His penknife was where it always was, in the back pocket of the jeans he hadn't got round to climbing out of. It wasn't designed as a weapon, mostly he used it for marking cuts in timber, but it was strong and it was sharp, and producing it would have made a casual mugger pause for thought. This man was not a casual mugger. If Horn dived for his back pocket, he'd kill him. Even if he managed to get it out, he'd have to open it before it would be any use; and when he did, it was still only a penknife. If he somehow managed to get it out and open and offer to fight with it, this man—this professional assassin— would laugh at him and *then* kill him.

He left the knife where it was. It couldn't help him. Probably nothing would help him, but it was worth trying a lie. He'd got good at lying these last four years. "No," he said, trying for the urgent cooperation of someone with nothing to hide. "He did a runner last night. I'm just minding—"

He never got the sentence finished. He'd been right about the gun. The outline of the man against the landing light, which had barely moved in the long seconds since it appeared in the doorway, moved now: not extravagantly, not flashily, but with an incisive speed that was awe-inspiring. Horn gasped and recoiled.

There wasn't much he was too slow for, but he was too slow

now. The intruder had chosen to use his weapon in a manner for which it had not been designed but was nonetheless highly effective—cripplingly effective, and all but silent. He palmed the ugly weapon and slapped Horn across the jaw with it.

Pain exploded through his face and ran like molten steel down his spine. His strong limbs went to string and his fit young body spun half a turn before crashing to the floor. The light had gone out before he hit the carpet.

CHAPTER 2

BUT HE WASN'T unconscious long. Pain drilling every tooth in his left jaw yanked him back. He lay in a fetal curl under the window, arms cradling his raging head. He heard himself whine like a kicked puppy, but his vision was worse than useless—a dark mist laced with shooting stars. He'd always thought that was a comic-strip invention, but like most clichés it was an accurate observation first.

He didn't know which way was up, he hardly knew what had happened, but he knew he had to get back on his feet. He didn't want to. He didn't want to move, for fear of making the pain worse, for fear of being hit again. But primordial instinct wanted him to live even more than it wanted to spare him pain, and it drove him back ruthlessly to the reality of that cold, unlit room and the killer he shared it with. If he went on lying here he was going to die on this square of grubby carpet, adding his blood to the sum of its uncertain stains. That was going to be his obituary: a packet of Shake 'n' Vac in his landlord's shopping cart.

Probably he was going to die anyway, but he had an element of choice about how. Nicky Horn had faced death many times, much more often than was reasonable for an otherwise rational man in peacetime. But he'd never faced it groveling on the floor, whining about being hurt. He put out a hand, groping for something he could use to pull himself up.

To his muddled surprise, someone helped. He still couldn't see anything but stars, but only the two of them were here, so it had to be the man who'd hit him. His reeling brain wasn't up to working out why: he let the strong hands gripping his shoulders lift him to his feet, and was too groggy to note that someone holding him with both hands must have put his gun away.

The man propped Horn against the wall and held him there, quite gently, with one hand in the middle of his chest. It wouldn't have stopped him from throwing a punch, but then it wasn't meant to. It was to stop him from sliding back down the wall. After a short contemplation the man leaned forward, peering into Horn's face. "Can you walk?"

Even Horn knew it wasn't solicitude. The man wanted to take him away from here, a house he shared with a dozen other people, to somewhere he could finish his job without fear of interruption, somewhere he could leave the detritus that it mightn't be found for weeks; and he wanted Horn to leave under his own steam in case someone saw them. The assault was carefully calculated to knock all the fight out of him without leaving him so incapable he'd need to be dragged, with the attendant risk—even at this time of night—of attracting attention. Horn went to shake his head, thought better of it, carefully mumbled, "No."

The man smiled. Horn couldn't see the smile but he could hear it in his voice. "I'm sure you can. I'll help." He draped Horn's arm over his shoulder, and that was how they went down the stairs, out into the dark street, and round the first corner to where an unremarkable navy blue saloon car was waiting. It might have taken a minute, no more. Anyone seeing them would have thought Horn was drunk, his killer a helpful friend.

Horn spent the time thinking—almost expecting—that something would happen. Someone would stop them, or a police patrol would swing by, or Horn would recover just enough of his strength to knee his assailant in the groin and leg it, trusting he could get back round the corner faster than a man nursing that most personal of hurts could draw his gun.

But none of those things happened. They reached the car. The man opened the back door. Horn planted an unsteady hand against the frame, as sure as death and taxes that if he allowed himself to be forced inside the game was over. "You don't have to do this," he mumbled, steering the words carefully past his throbbing teeth. "Tell him you couldn't find me."

"And what? You think he'll pay me anyway? You think my employer will worry if my children don't get their ski trip this year? I'm sorry. But this is how I make my living."

"I don't deserve this," insisted Horn weakly. "I haven't done anything to deserve it."

"No? But you see, I don't care." Quite calmly the man exchanged his grip on Horn's arm for a handful of his hair and banged his forehead smartly on the top of the car. The shooting stars took flight again like a flock of startled starlings, the pain in his face exploded like fireworks, and as Horn's knees buckled the man folded him expertly onto the backseat.

Then something unexpected happened.

Because in all honesty, nothing that had happened up to this point had been in any way unpredictable. It had only been a matter of time. Horn had run as long as he could, laid up as carefully as he could; but he'd always known that one of Hanratty's dogs, faster or keener or more persistent than the others, would find him one day. Today was that day. He couldn't honestly claim to be surprised.

But the smooth inevitability of it seemed now to meet an obstacle. The car door that should have closed with the crisp snap of a hangman's trapdoor remained open, the engine silent. Instead, after a moment, he heard voices.

"The sensible thing," said the one he hadn't heard before, "would be to leave him here and drive away."

There was a brief pause in which Horn almost heard the sound of mental cogs changing gear. Then Hanratty's man said mildly, "I don't know what you mean. There's no problem here."

"No? Let's ask him."

The man with the gun hadn't forgotten he had it. He just wasn't ready to draw it in front of someone he hadn't come here to kill. He moved proprietorially between Horn and the new arrival. "I've got a better idea. Let's not."

"It doesn't look to me as if he wants to come with you."

"He doesn't." A light, inconsequential laugh. "But his wife wants him home just the same."

"He isn't married."

Horn heard the elevated eyebrow. "You know him?"

"Never met him in my life. But I know a lie when I hear one."

When his lie has been rumbled, a wise man stops lying. This wise man's voice dropped a couple of tones. He wasn't trying to sound menacing. He didn't have to, any more than a tiger has to try.

"You don't know what you're getting involved in. So I'll tell you what you need to do. Turn round and walk away."

The other man laughed. There was gravel in it. "Oh, I've a pretty good idea what's going on. If I walk away, he's going to end up dead."

"If you don't, maybe you will."

"Or maybe he survives, and I survive, and you die in prison for all the times you did this and got away with it."

A longer silence this time. When Hanratty's man spoke again, for the first time Horn heard a fractional uncertainty. "You know *me*?"

"Not your name. Not where to find you—though I know where to find people *like* you. But I know what you do, and how you do it. What's the preferred term these days? You're a mechanic—a hit man, a professional killer. You aren't going to compromise your own safety doing your job. Martyrdom is for people who espouse causes, and you don't believe in causes. You're a practical man. If you let him go tonight, you can find him again tomorrow. If you don't, things are going to get messy, and noisy, right now. You'll have gone to a lot of trouble to keep them clean and quiet, so I'm pretty sure you won't want that. But whether I start shouting or you start shooting, you're going to have an audience in just a few seconds from now. Unless you leave."

Incredulously, Horn began to realize that it could actually happen. That an assassin hard enough to appear on Tommy Hanratty's radar just might back down before the extraordinary courage of a passerby. Not because he couldn't take him too—of course he could. But he was a professional, he had to think about the next job and the one after that, and to do them he had to keep a low profile. He didn't have to let Horn go—he just had to let him go for now. In all probability Horn was still going to die. But there was now a chance that he wasn't going to die tonight.

The pause could only have been a few seconds. It wrung Horn like the rack. Finally the man said, faintly aggrieved, "Bloody amateurs!"

The other man, the passerby, said softly, "You don't know that. You don't know who I am or what I can do. You can gamble everything on a guess. Or you can do the sensible thing, which is haul him out of there and drive away. That way there's always another day, another chance."

A few seconds more and it happened. A yank on his ankle landed Horn on his back in the wet road. For the first time he could see the two figures, dark against the rain-reflected glitter of the streetlights. They were about three meters apart. Far enough that the only weapons that would reach were bullets and words. Still he could see no faces.

But the one nearest to him got back in his car and shut the door. Horn heard the quiet electric whir of the window. "I won't forget this."

"I don't imagine any of us will," said the other man calmly. "But I'll keep quiet about it if you will."

The engine started and the car moved off, slowly at first, then gaining speed. Then there were just the two of them—Horn too weak with concussion and relief to clamber to his feet, and the man to whom he owed his life.

Who now turned back toward the main street and said casually over his shoulder, "Good luck, then."

"W-w-w-?" It wasn't just the concussion making Horn's head spin. "Where are you going? Who are you? Why . . . ?"

The man looked down at him with the same admixture of indulgence and exasperation he'd have worn if his puppy had fallen down the coalhole. "Do you want to pick one?"

The other man had been bad news—the worst—but his appearance had not come as a surprise. Horn had known he, or someone like him, would turn up sometime. He'd known why, and he'd known what to expect of him. What was he to make of a complete stranger risking his own neck to offer him protection?

He did as he was told and picked one. But first he crawled on his hands and knees to a handy bollard and hauled himself to his feet, and leaned against it to stop the world swaying. "You saved my life. Why?"

The man thought for a moment. "I suppose, because I hoped it was worth saving."

The dull fear that had given way to tremulous hope was now yielding to a kind of uncomprehending rage, because none of this made any sense to Nicky Horn. When a large part of his world had collapsed about him, he'd consoled himself with the thought that—unlike most men—at least he knew how and why he would die. Now even that seemed to have been snatched from him. He felt he was owed an explanation. "You can't know that! You don't know me."

The man moved a couple of paces closer. They stared at one another by the limited light reaching the side street. Horn saw a tall, rangy individual in a long, dark coat, short hair the color of moonlight. Narrow, clean-shaven face. A bit of an intellectual, you'd have said, if you hadn't just seen him face down a hired killer.

For his part, the man saw someone physically and emotionally battered, with blood on his face and road dirt on his clothes, struggling to keep his feet both actually and metaphorically. A young man in his midtwenties, not tall but sturdy, strong. Dark hair, overdue a trim, falling in his face in rats' tails courtesy of the rain. No coat, and no shoes. He didn't look as if he'd fallen in the gutter. He looked as if he'd been living in it.

His voice was gruff, plainly well-educated, and laced in equal quantities with humor and irritation. "You're—what?—twenty-six, twenty-seven years old? It doesn't seem beyond the realms of possibility that somewhere in the next fifty years you might do something of value to someone. In fact, you might make it a kind of New Life's Resolution. That one day you'll help someone else who has no one left to turn to."

"He could have killed you!" Disbelief sent the words soaring. "I thought he was going to kill you."

The man shook his head. "No one was paying him to kill me. And he couldn't kill you and leave me standing here, so he couldn't kill you either. Today. Tomorrow will be different. If I were you, I'd try to sort out my differences with whoever sent him."

"I wish I could," said Horn feelingly.

"Too much water under the bridge?"

"Too much blood."

The man's head was tilted to one side as he studied Nicky Horn, apparently unsure what to make of him. Something about the tilt was familiar. Yes—the mirror. The man in the car who met his eyes before looking away to check his mirror. "I've seen you before," said Horn.

"That's possible," the man agreed negligently.

"Last night. Outside the sandwich bar."

"Yes?"

"You live round here?"

"I was on my way home."

Though Horn wasn't on top form mentally, he could see the problem with that. "So what are you still doing here five hours later?"

The man chuckled, enjoying Horn's confusion. "You're accusing me of loitering? Of lowering the tone of the neighborhood? You wish I'd taken my cheese-on-rye and gone home?"

The whole tenor of the conversation was troubling Horn. It was as if the man was enjoying a joke at his expense. They'd both come close to dying, Horn closest, but the other man closer than he'd probably ever been before, and he thought it was funny.

Then he realized what the man had been doing here. The only possible explanation—for his presence in this run-down district, for the time he'd spent here, for his being on the street at three in the morning. It even explained the mood of recklessness that had led him to intervene in a situation he should have passed with an averted eye. "You were with a hooker."

The man laughed out loud. "That's right, Officer, you've got me bang to rights. Oh, the shame! Please don't tell my wife. The shock would kill my mother." He looked round. "Now, if we've got that out of the way, and if you're not too embarrassed to be seen with an old curb-crawler, can I give you a lift anywhere?"

Horn blinked, waved a hand that was still not quite steady. "My room's only up there . . ."

"Your room," said the man evenly. "Your room where a hired killer found you. You're planning on going back there, are you?"

"I . . ." If his head had been a bit clearer he wouldn't have considered it. He didn't own so many clothes that leaving them behind would be much loss. His toolkit was another matter. He needed it to work. If he couldn't work, he couldn't buy a new one. He also needed his boots. "I have to get a couple of things. If you can wait, I won't be a minute. If you can't, thanks anyway." It wasn't much to say to a man he owed his life to, but it was sincere.

The man shrugged. "I'll wait."

Horn got as far as the hallway. But the stairs defeated him. While he was regarding them owlishly, wondering if he'd wake the whole house by going up on his hands and knees, a hand on his shoulder moved him quite gently aside. "Tell me what you need."

He was too grateful to argue. "The toolbag's just inside the door. My jacket's on the hook. My wallet's in the pocket, and my boots are probably under the bed. Everything else I can leave."

In fact the man took a moment longer and threw everything he could see into the haversack Horn used as a suitcase. He reappeared carrying it in one hand and the toolbag in the other, a combined load that would have made most men half his age think twice. But he passed Horn briskly and threw the gear onto the backseat of his car. "Get in."

Horn did as he was told.

The man drove off immediately, without waiting for directions. They'd already pushed their luck further than it could be expected to stretch—anything they had to say to one another could be said as they drove. It was time to be somewhere else.

He crossed the center of town, cut through the park, circled a couple of roundabouts. With no sign of pursuit, he glanced at the young man in the seat beside him. "How's the face?"

"Sore," admitted Horn.

"There's ibuprofen in the glove box. It might help a bit."

A double brandy might have helped more, but even if one had been on offer Horn couldn't have risked dulling his rattled wits any further. He took the ibuprofen, struggling to swallow it with no water and teeth too painful to chew.

"Is there somewhere you can go where you'll be safe?"

Horn grinned mirthlessly into the night, a savage slash of white across his face. "Not for long."

"This has happened before?"

"Oh yeah."

"So it'll happen again."

Horn nodded.

"But you're still alive."

"Born lucky, I guess," muttered Horn.

"You were lucky tonight. What about next time?"

Horn gave a sigh of infinite weariness and let his aching head rock back against the headrest. "Who knows? Who cares?"

The man went on looking at him almost too long for someone driving a car. Then he cranked his eyes back to the road. "Do you want to tell me what it's all about?"

Horn shook his head, wished he hadn't. "Not particularly."

The man breathed in and out a few times, with mounting annoyance. "You can't just say that and then expect me to leave you at a bus stop. Whatever's brought you to this point, there has to be a way forward. What about the police?"

"It's not a police matter," said Horn.

"Somebody's trying to kill you. That *makes* it a police matter!"

"Just . . . let me out near the motorway. I'll hitch. I'll break the trail. I'll be all right."

"How long for?"

Horn managed a grim little chuckle. "The rest of my life."

He knew all the roads in and out of this town, as he'd known all the roads in and out of every town where he'd broken his endless journey. The car missed two turnings for the motorway. "Where are we going?"

The man didn't look at him. "My place."

"No."

"Till I can figure out what to do with you."

"No," Horn said again, with as much insistence as he could muster. "It isn't safe."

"You know somewhere better?"

"I don't mean for *me*!"

The man considered for a moment. "It's probably safer than you think. It was designed to keep people out. It'll do for what's left of tonight."

They drove for what seemed like hours. Not so much oblivious of the danger on his heels as unable to do much about it, Horn slept for a lot of it, his sore head rocking gently against the headrest. When he woke, disturbed by the sudden grate of gravel under the wheels, sunrise was painting the horizon with streaks of oyster and pink. And silhouetting . . .

He sat up straighter, knuckled his eyes, and looked again. It was still there, and still what he'd first thought. Which went some way to explaining the last thing the man had said to him before he fell asleep, although it made everything else that had happened even more incomprehensible. Chills played up and down his spine. He said in a harsh, flat voice, "Who the hell lives in a castle?"

The man chuckled complacently. "Rich people. Welcome to Birkholmstead—*this* Englishman's home."

"You're rich?"

"Rich enough."

So much to lose . . . "Am I supposed to know who you are? Royalty—a duke or something?"

The man laughed. "I'm not famous. The only way you'd know my name is if you study the financial pages very closely."

"What is your name?"

"Robert McKendrick."

"And you're, what, a banker?"

"Near enough."

Horn looked at the castle again. All right, it wasn't a big castle, but you couldn't have described it as anything else. It was constructed of honey-colored stone and rose from a compact footprint up through five stories. The front door was at head height—a powerful defense when the place was built, now approached by a broad flight of steps. Beyond a wide graveled terrace there were gardens. "I thought the stock market had pretty much crashed."

There was something ruthless about McKendrick's grin. "Lose a lot of your portfolio, did you?"

Horn bristled. He wasn't stupid. There was a reason he was living out of a haversack. Even if there hadn't been, it would have been offensive for a man who lived the way this one did to look down his nose at someone who didn't. "I never went in for investments. I didn't trust the bastards in charge."

McKendrick laughed again, but he didn't argue the point. He looked at the clock on the dashboard. "Almost seven. Beth'll be up by now. Or if she isn't, she will be in a minute." He blew the horn as the drive curved along the front of the house.

"Is Beth your wife?"

"My daughter."

After the car came to a halt Horn stayed where he was,

slumped in the leather embrace of the passenger seat. When McKendrick got out, he made no move to follow. "You shouldn't have brought me to your home. To your family's home."

The older man made a dismissive gesture, half irritable shrug, half impatient shake of the head. "I told you, you're safe here."

Horn's patience snapped. He owed this man a lot, but there's more than one way to repay a debt. One is to be meek and agreeable and do what you're told. Another is to do what's right. "And I told you," he shouted, "I'm not safe anywhere. And *you're* not safe while I'm here. Neither's your daughter. Maybe you've some kind of a death wish, maybe you're entitled to gamble with your own life, but you're not entitled to gamble with someone else's. Your own daughter's, for God's sake!

"Mr. McKendrick, I'm grateful for what you did. But I don't want your death on my conscience, and I sure as hell don't want your daughter's!" Finally Horn got out of the car, hauled his bags off the backseat. He looked around. All he could see were fields. "Tell me where we are and I'll make my own way from here."

As McKendrick watched him over the top of the car, an odd combination of expressions flickered across his face. Surprise and annoyance, because he wasn't used to being contradicted. In spite of that, a reluctant respect because of course it would have been easier for Horn to accept his reassurances and stay. Something like grim amusement, as if they were playing a game of which only one of them knew the rules. And perhaps just a little human sympathy, because whatever else his visitor was, he was scared and hurt, and lonely, and a long way from anything or anyone he dared think of as home.

McKendrick's tone softened. "Let me show you something."

He had a second fob on his key ring, beside the one that locked his car. He pointed it at the front of the castle and thumbed the button. Immediately a metallic sound, quiet and purposeful, surrounded the house, and Horn was astonished to see steel shutters fall behind the windows. All the windows on the ground, first, and second floors. Within about ten seconds the little castle was locked down.

"I do take my security seriously," McKendrick said. "If I'd thought for one moment that helping you would compromise my daughter's safety, I'd have turned my back on you and walked away without a second glance. Do you believe me?"

Horn did. But he was no closer to understanding. "Then why—?"

He was interrupted by a furious shout from a window immediately above the lockdown. "What the hell's going on? Mack, is that you?"

Immediately McKendrick raised his voice in contrite reply. "Sorry, Beth, I didn't mean to scare you. Just testing. We're coming in now." He thumbed the fob again, and the steel shutters rolled quietly back into their casements. He led the way up the stone steps to the heavy oak front door. After a moment's hesitation Horn followed.

But as McKendrick reached for it, the door flew open and a young woman stood barring it with her body and her fury. Her eyes blazed. She was barefoot on the stone flags, and her long chestnut hair and the dressing gown she'd pulled loosely over her pajamas were tossing in the dawn wind. She looked like a recruiting poster for the Home Guard.

"What the holy hell are you playing at?" she yelled, beside herself with anger, oblivious of the stranger hovering warily in the background. "It's seven o'clock in the morning! I'm here on my own. What am I supposed to think when the house goes to DEFCON Three?" Finally she noticed they had company. It did nothing for her temper, or her voice, which soared like an eagle. "And who the blue blinding blazes . . . ?"

And there she stopped. Dead; as if one of them had slapped her. Her expression froze, except that her eyes saucered with an incredulity so absolute that for a moment it drove the anger out. But only a moment. When it surged back, it came like a tsunami, and she hauled her dressing gown about her and spun on her bare heel and disappeared wordlessly back into the castle, her whole vanishing body stiff with fury and disbelief.

"I don't think she was expecting company," said McKendrick with masterly understatement. "Come inside. Let's see what we can do for your face."

There were no suits of armor. Horn was vaguely disappointed. His only experience of how the rich lived was gleaned from country-house mysteries on late-night TV, and he was sure that suits of armor figured prominently. And not so much computer screens and an exercise bicycle.

McKendrick saw where Horn was looking and grinned. "Not very appropriate, I know. But then, where in a fourteenth-century castle would be?"

When they were inside, McKendrick keyed numbers into a pad, automatically, as if he did it all the time. Horn didn't try, but he was fairly sure that if he'd wanted to leave then he wouldn't have been able to. He followed the master of Birkholmstead through the stone-flagged hallway into a surprisingly small and comfortable sitting room.

McKendrick pointed at a sofa. "Park yourself, I'll get the kettle on." He disappeared through another door, from which came the unmistakable sounds of crockery. But he returned with not a breakfast tray but a first-aid kit.

In truth, there wasn't much that needed doing. The blood from Horn's nose had dried on his face, and he looked better once that was cleaned off. The bruising along his jaw was already purpling, and nothing but time would resolve it. "Any broken teeth?"

Horn explored carefully. "I don't think so."

"In that case, coffee will do as much good as anything." McKendrick took away the first-aid kit and came back with breakfast—a pot of coffee, toast, marmalade. Three cups. "Beth'll be down in a minute."

He supposed McKendrick knew his own daughter, but Horn hadn't got the impression she was in any hurry to meet him formally. He took the coffee and let the bitter steam work its magic in his throbbing sinuses.

Finally McKendrick said what Horn had been expecting him to say for the last four hours. "Whether or not you want to tell me what's going on, you owe me an explanation."

"Because you saved my neck?"

"It isn't a good enough reason?"

It wasn't a bad one. Horn could still have refused to answer. He'd been accused of a lot of things in the last few years—rudeness was hardly a blip on the radar. But the man *had* saved him, at considerable risk to himself, and Horn had always had a strong sense of fair play. Even if it had only delayed the inevitable, McKendrick's intervention earned him something.

Still Horn hesitated. He wasn't fabricating a lie: he was trying to shape a couple of tidy sentences that would outline the history between Hanratty and himself without going into all the gory details. It was taking time because he hadn't even tried to put it into words for years, since policemen stopped asking questions about it.

Finally he said, "Someone died. On a mountain. His father blames me."

The thin brow above McKendrick's hawkish eye climbed. "So he sent a hit man after you?"

Horn gave a weary shrug. "He's not a very nice man."

"No, really?" McKendrick's voice dropped a tone. "Is he right? Was it your fault?"

Horn was too tired to lie. "Probably."

"What was his name? The boy who fell."

"Patrick." Horn said it as if they'd been close.

"And it's his father who's after you," observed McKendrick. "Not the authorities. So the police accept that it was an accident but the father doesn't. Why not?"

Horn was going to tell him. It was a matter of public record, and nothing McKendrick did with the knowledge was capable of hurting Horn any more. But he didn't get the chance.

He hadn't heard the door behind him open, but he heard it shut. When he looked round, Beth McKendrick, dressed now and with her hair pulled back into a thick, ragged bunch, was staring at him with undisguised disgust. "Because he did what no climber ever does," she said, her voice vibrant with a chilly rage. "Ever. Not even to save his own neck."

Her head jerked and she glared at her father. "Don't you

know who he is? You bring him to our house, and you don't even know who he is? One day you must try reading that bit of your newspaper wrapped round the financial pages."

McKendrick was looking between the two of them—the battered young man on his sofa, the angry young woman behind it—as if this development were nearly as fascinating as a Mexican standoff with a professional killer. "All right, tell me. Who is he?"

Horn said, through tight lips, "My name's Nicky Horn."

Beth gave a little snort of laughter with absolutely no amusement in it. "The tabloids called him Anarchy Horn. He's the man who cut Patrick Hanratty's rope."

CHAPTER 3

THE SILENCE went on and on. A glacial silence. Beth said nothing to break it because everything she'd had to say she'd said in those two sentences. Even with time to think, she knew they couldn't be improved on. Horn said nothing because he had nothing to say. Everyone and his dog knew the story and had an opinion about what had happened on Anarchy Ridge above the Little Horse River. Horn hadn't been left with a lot, but he still had too much pride to beg forgiveness of total strangers.

McKendrick said nothing because he seemed to be waiting. As if he thought Beth's revelation were an opening gambit rather than a last word. But no further information was forthcoming, so finally he looked at Horn. "I notice you're not denying it."

Horn turned to face him, and it seemed to take more effort than even the residual concussion might have explained. "Why would I deny it? *She* knows who I am. Most people know who I am. Most people reckon they know what happened."

"You're saying they don't?"

"I'm saying none of the fireside experts has the faintest idea what they're talking about." Horn's eyes were hot, red-rimmed with resentment. "Climbers know. What it's like in the mountains, where you put your life in other people's hands so often, so totally, that it stops seeming like a big deal. You hold them, they hold you. It's the norm. You trust one another. Then something goes wrong and suddenly it's a big deal again. Other climbers have the right to judge me. People in pubs haven't. Nor have people who care so much about their own safety that they live in castles."

"Actually—" began McKendrick, but Beth interrupted him.

"Other climbers *have* judged you."

The flash of desperate anger died in Horn's eyes as quickly as it had flared. She wasn't telling him anything he didn't know. He lived with the knowledge; the knowledge was like a worm in his gut, eating away even when he was asleep. He growled, "They weren't there."

"Well, that's true enough," said Beth McKendrick tartly. "The only one there was you, which is why Patrick Hanratty's buried in a glacier in Alaska. Anyone else—*anyone*—would have got him out of there, or died trying. But it was you. And you cut his rope."

"I held him for three hours," gritted Nicky Horn. "I couldn't hold him any longer. I thought by then he was dead. That I was holding a dead man."

"But you would say that, wouldn't you?" spat Beth. "And we've only your word for the three hours. Maybe you got tired after the first ten minutes. When you couldn't pull him up and he couldn't help himself. Maybe that's when you got your knife out. Maybe you thought, since that was how it was likely to end anyway, there was no point straining yourself first."

"It was hours," repeated Horn. There was something odd, thought McKendrick, about the way Horn spoke. Almost mechanical. As if he'd told the story so often that the words came automatically now, almost without his thinking about them. But that was just the words. Behind them, in the pits of his eyes, the emotion was still raw—as raw as if it had happened yesterday. "The wind was whipping the snow off the ridge around us. He was hanging on the end of a rope in the wind and the snow. He hadn't answered me, and I hadn't felt him move, for hours. When I cut him loose, I thought he was dead. I still think that."

He didn't say aloud, "I have to," but McKendrick heard it as clearly as if he had.

Beth's voice dropped softer. "But you're the man who killed his partner rather than risk being pulled off the mountain by him. Why would anyone believe a word you say?"

Incredibly, Horn laughed. "They don't," he said, as if she'd missed the point of a rather simple joke. "They never have. But they can't prove anything different, so they have to accept it. So do you. Patrick's death was an accident—misadventure, a combination of recklessness and bad luck. You can think what you like, but the inquest said I wasn't responsible."

"But his father," murmured McKendrick, putting the pieces together quickly now, "was no more convinced by the findings of an Alaskan coroner than my daughter appears to be."

"Tommy Hanrattty's a criminal and a thug," snarled Horn. "If I'd done everything I've been accused of doing, I'll still be kept waiting at the gates of hell while Old Nick ushers Tommy Hanratty inside."

"Is he serious? About killing you?"

Horn stared at McKendrick, wide-eyed with disbelief. "You were there last night. Did that guy look to you like he was kidding?"

"Well—no," McKendrick said slowly. "I suppose he didn't."

Finally Beth seemed to realize that, consumed by her anger, she'd missed a large chunk of what was going on. "What guy? Where did you go last night? Where did you find . . . *this*"—she invested the word with infinite contempt—"and why did you bring it here?"

McKendrick summarized what had happened in a handful of brief, simplistic sentences that probably raised more questions than they answered. At least, the way Beth was looking at him didn't suggest that now she understood any better. It took her a moment to find a voice. "You risked your life? For *that*?"

McKendrick shrugged. "I didn't know who he was, then," he said reasonably. "I'm not sure it would have made a difference if I had."

She quite literally didn't know what to say to him. She felt riven by betrayal but couldn't tell him why. She might have tried but for the fear of what would come through if she opened the floodgates. All she could manage was a stunned expression and a few breathless, uncomprehending words. "You could have died. You could have died and left me alone. For that."

Horn hauled himself stiffly off the sofa. "I get the message: you don't want me here. Point me in the direction of anywhere I'll have heard of and I'll leave. You'll never see me again and there's no reason you should waste another thought on me, let alone an argument. Thanks for what you did," he told McKendrick, "but she's right, you shouldn't have got involved. Do the"—he wiggled his thumb on an imaginary keypad—"thing with the locks and let me out.

"Just for the record, though," he added, his gaze swiveling round to Beth, "Patrick Hanratty was my friend. My best friend.

I did everything I could to save him. It wasn't enough. Nothing I could have done would have been enough. If I could have bought his life with mine, I would have done."

If he was looking for some hint of understanding, some glimmer of compassion, some brief acknowledgment of their shared humanity and the knowledge that everyone makes mistakes and it's the intention by which an act should be judged rather than its consequences, then he'd come to the wrong counter.

Beth McKendrick's lip twisted in a sneer of infinite disdain. "You think you're your own harshest critic? Not while I'm alive you're not. You think that anyone else, put in the same position, would have done as you did? Don't flatter yourself. Patrick had a lot of friends, from a lot further back than you. Any one of us would have died on that mountain rather than leave him there."

Everything else he'd expected—the sneer, the contempt, nothing new there—but that he hadn't. "You knew him?"

"Yes, I knew him. We were at university together." She said it with a kind of unconscious hubris. "We were both in the climbing club. He was way out of my league, but we did several routes together. And guess what? Every time we climbed—*every* time—the same number of people came down as went up."

Something changed in Nicky Horn's eyes. It had been his last redoubt, the belief that other climbers—who understood and accepted the risks, who could imagine finding themselves in the same cruel quandary—might judge him less harshly than the general public, whose view of what happened was shaped by tabloid headlines consisting largely of exclamation marks. If he was wrong about that, then he was entirely alone—a pariah, unforgiven and unforgivable.

The only way to survive with the whole world against you is to fight.

He'd been running for four years. From Tommy Hanratty, but also from the past. Now there was nowhere left to go. This woman with her iron eyes had nailed his soul to the wall. She knew who he was, she knew the story of what he'd done—she thought she knew everything. But if there was nowhere left to hide, there was no reason left to try. In so far as he could be honest with anyone, he could be honest with her. It might not do much to salve her hatred of him, but that wasn't the point. Hatred is a corrosive, like acid splashed on skin. Self-hatred is like injecting it into a vein. For once he wanted to stand up like a man and hit back, because if he didn't he'd go to his grave without even trying to set the record straight. Or no, not that—setting the record straight was the last thing he wanted, he'd thrown his life away to avoid setting the record straight. But there were things he needed to say to someone, and she'd do.

McKendrick saw him stiffen, the strong muscles drawing his sturdy, compact frame into a state of balanced tension. In such a state he could have crimped his fingertips on a ledge of rock and swung out over the void, feeling the fear but doing it anyway—*knowing* he could do it anyway. Adrenaline fed into his blood not in a wild rush but like fuel injected into a highly tuned engine, equipping him first to face his demons and then to deal with them. To conquer them or die trying.

"Patrick Hanratty was my friend," he said again. There was a tremor in his voice that McKendrick thought Horn was unaware of, that McKendrick attributed not so much to fear or even anger as the absolute need to get this said. Horn had taken everything Beth had to throw at him, and now it was his turn. There was the sense that he'd been waiting for it for a long time. "More than that, he was my climbing partner. You knew him at university? Wow, I'm impressed. I bet you went punting on the river and everything, didn't you? I bet you wore matching scarves.

"But it wasn't you he went to Alaska with. Or to Utah, or the Cascades, or even the Alps." McKendrick almost fancied he felt a cold wind breathe through the little room as Horn spoke. "When the climbing was going to be hard, and dangerous, and he knew as we all do that if he fell there'd only be one chance for someone to catch him, it wasn't you he wanted on his rope. It was me.

"We climbed in places where no one could help if it all went wrong—where no one would even know. And it *did* go wrong. Not once, but again and again. He owed his life to me more times than either of us could count, and I owed mine to him. And we never, ever wore matching scarves."

He sucked in a hard breath. "What happened on Anarchy Ridge wasn't a fluke. It didn't come out of nowhere and take us by surprise. When you climb the way we did, pioneering our own routes, our own *mountains* sometimes, every time you go out you know there's a real risk you're going to come up against something you can't deal with. Hell, it's *why* we went out. He could have stayed with the university climbing club and got really good on indoor walls and the routes that figure in the guidebooks, the ones where you're likely to meet someone's mom on the way down. He could have done that with you, couldn't he? But he didn't want to. It wasn't enough for him. He wanted to be up there at the sharp end, finding routes and making them, and for that neither you nor any of his university friends were good enough. For that he needed me.

"You know why? Because I'm good." There wasn't much pride

in the way he said it: mostly it was bitterness. "I'm strong, and I'm savvy, and I don't give up easily. I can take the pain, and the exhaustion, and still want to go on—still find some way of going on. Patrick was the same. Apart from the university thing, of course. He talked posher than me. He was cleverer than me. But up there, where the wind and the ice don't much care about your accent or the letters after your name, we were pretty much alike. Most of the time"—the most fractional of catches—"I knew what he was thinking, what he was going to do next.

"We hardly talked when we were climbing. We didn't have to. I always knew what he was going to try because it was always what I'd have done in the same situation." He took a moment then to get the words in the right order. "That's what I did on Anarchy Ridge. I did what he'd have done for me in the same situation. I did my best. I held him for as long as I could. When I couldn't hold him anymore, and the only alternative was dying with him, I let him go."

He moistened his bruised lips. "If you think you can make me feel worse about that, you're wrong. If you think you can make me wonder if it was the right decision, you're wrong about that too. I know it was the right decision. If I'd been hanging on his rope, it's what I'd have wanted Patrick to do. I'd have wanted him to do everything in his power to save me—and when it wasn't enough, I'd have wanted him to save himself. To survive. To get home and tell people what happened. That I'd got the death I wanted. That I'd rather have lived, but if I had to die, that was the place to do it. That I never wanted to be buried anywhere other than a mountain glacier.

"Mind," he added as a sarcastic footnote, "I never went to university. I don't think you can do a PhD in joinery. Pity, really. Maybe if I'd got a PhD, I'd behave more like an officer and a gentleman, and see the point of having two people dead on a mountain when you could just have one."

It was the most talking Horn had done since McKendrick had met him. It was the nearest thing to eloquence he'd heard from him. It made him view Horn in a rather different light. It didn't make him change his mind about anything, though.

It had more of an effect on Beth. She'd gone very white. Now a flush of pink stole up her cheeks. She opened her mouth to reply but no words came. As if, McKendrick thought critically, she were willing to beat a cowering dog but not one that might snap back.

But he remembered how upset she'd been by Patrick Hanratty's death. She'd hardly talked about it—they had never, thought McKendrick ruefully, been great talkers—but first the news and then the details that emerged over the following weeks had swept the feet from under her. As if she and young Hanratty had been better friends than he'd realized.

She stood frozen, staring at Horn's battered, embattled face as if he'd stepped out of one of her nightmares and she didn't know what to do about him. Then she clamped her jaw shut, turned abruptly and left the room, slamming the door behind her so that the air in the little sitting room went on reverberating for seconds.

After a moment McKendrick said mildly, "She always used to do that when she was cross. You wouldn't believe the number of hinges I've had to replace."

Horn gave a little pant like a hunted fox as some of the tension left him. "I think," he said carefully, "she was more than cross."

"She was upset. It's understandable, in the circumstances."

"You reckon?" drawled Horn with heavy irony. "What in God's name were you thinking? You knew she was a friend of Patrick's, you must have realized how bringing me here was going to hurt her. Why would you do that?"

McKendrick chuckled. "I'm sorry, Nicky—Nicky?—but you're nowhere near as famous as you think you are. I didn't recognize you. Sure, I'd heard the story—of course I had, Beth was at university with the boy who died. But it was all years ago. I probably saw your face in the papers at the time, but I'd no reason to remember it. I'd no reason to suppose Beth would know you from Adam."

McKendrick leaned forward to refill his cup from the coffee-pot. "So that's what it was all about—the guy with the gun. Patrick Hanratty's father sent him. And he's still after you four years later." He thought about that. "A bit obsessive, I'd have thought. I mean, yes, it was his son, he was entitled to hold a grudge. But if you go in for risk sports, sometimes you draw the short straw. I'd have thought that was part of the deal. I can see he might strike you off his Christmas-card list, but a hired killer seems a bit much."

"I told you," growled Horn, "he's not a nice man. I mean, really. He runs one of Dublin's crime syndicates. He scared the shit out of Patrick—from when he was old enough to leave home he stayed as far away from his dad as he could. He bullied him as a child, used his fists on him as a teenager. He's got some nerve now pretending Patrick was the apple of his eye."

"He isn't doing it for Patrick. He's doing it because someone took something away from him. From *him*—Tommy Hanratty. If I'd boosted a slab of his cocaine, he'd have called the same guy. Nobody takes anything from Tommy Hanratty."

McKendrick was nodding slowly. "I still think four years is long enough to make a point. Have you tried talking to him?"

Horn looked at him as if he were mad. "*Talking* to him? He

sent a hired gun after me! He wants me dead, and he doesn't care who knows it. It's the worst-kept secret in criminology. If I went to his house, he'd do it himself. If he saw me in the street, he'd run me down in his car. Tonight wasn't the first time he's got close. This is how I've been living since the police lost interest in me. Because Tommy Hanratty is willing to do anything, pay anything, gamble anything, on seeing me dead. I wouldn't know how to begin talking him out of that."

"I could have a word with him."

Horn laughed aloud at the sheer effrontery of it. "No, you won't have a word with him. You'll keep your head down, and your shutters up, and your drawbridge in the upright position, and hope Tommy Hanratty never hears your name. If he ever gets the idea that it was you who came between him and having my heart in a plastic bag tonight, he'll come after you too. And your daughter, and anyone else he thinks you might care about. And you'll be easier to find than me."

"Oh, I think I can handle Mr. Hanratty." McKendrick smiled lazily.

"No, you can't," insisted Horn. "He doesn't play by your rules. He doesn't play by *any* rules. I'm sure you're a hard man in the City, and the closest thing your club has had to a rakehell since Byron got blackballed, but you're not in Tommy Hanratty's league. No one is. He hurts people for fun. When he's seriously pissed off, he does things you've never dreamed of, even after a lobster supper. You don't want him doing them to you, or to Beth."

"That's true," allowed McKendrick. "I'm not that happy about letting him do them to you, either."

"I am not your responsibility," yelled Horn, beside himself

with exasperation. "You've done enough already. I don't know why you got involved, and I don't know why we're still arguing about this when I've told you who I am and who Tommy Hanratty is. But you'll regret it for the rest of your life if you don't let me get on my way right now. You bought me some time, and I'm grateful for that. Now let me use it.

"He hasn't given up—the guy with the gun. He never did before, he hasn't this time. He's still looking. If I'm here when he catches up with me, it's going to be another of those inexplicable country-house murders that the Sunday papers love because it's rich people coming to a sticky end and no one's ever going to know why. He'll kill me, and you, and Beth, and he'll burn the house down, and he'll make it look like something quite different. As if maybe I broke in, and we killed one another in the struggle."

It seemed he'd finally found some words, evoked an image, that resonated with McKendrick. He had no reply. He stood for a moment, blinking stupidly, as though he'd just realized this wasn't a corporate team-building exercise, some kind of an elaborate game—a treasure hunt where the first one back to the hotel with a policeman's helmet gets the magnum of champers. As if he'd thought Horn had been exaggerating the danger, and now he wasn't sure.

Horn pressed his advantage, momentarily forgetting what winning the argument would mean. "Your stone walls and your steel shutters won't keep him out. Most of the people he goes after have them too. People as good at their job as this man cost a lot of money, and that means the people who hire them and most of the people they're sent after have lots of money too. Except me." He gave a mirthless grin.

"But even that sort of money won't buy everything. There isn't enough of it, there never would be, to stop someone like him. Once he took the job, it was a matter of professional pride for him to finish it. His reputation is everything to him—he'll do whatever's necessary to protect it. The stone walls and the shutters will slow him down but they won't stop him. Nothing will stop him.

"I can keep ahead of him. I have done this far, I can keep doing. For a while longer, anyway. Maybe I can run far enough and fast enough that he'll never catch up with me."

"And maybe you can't," said McKendrick levelly.

"That isn't your problem," insisted Horn. "Keeping yourself, and Beth, safe—that's your problem. And the thing about castles is, you pull up the drawbridge and immediately you're out of options. All you can do is sit there and wait to see what the other guy's going to do.

"Mr. McKendrick, what you did back there was a hell of a thing. You risked your life for someone you didn't even know. You risked losing all this"—Horn gave a jerky wave, encompassing the whole of the McKendrick estate with one unsteady gesture—"for a stranger. Whatever happens now won't alter that. Don't keep tempting fate until the old bitch bites your hand off."

McKendrick went on looking at him much too long, and Horn couldn't read his expression. Something was happening behind the cool gray eyes, but Horn couldn't tell what, or even if it was good or bad. But he knew that if McKendrick had been going to back down he'd have done it then, while the images of violence were vivid in his mind's eye. Once he started to think about it, he'd convince himself there were alternatives—that he was a clever enough man, a rich enough man, to find alternatives.

Horn gave up. He let the air out of his lungs in an audible sigh, weary and defeated. Without the starch of adrenaline his whole body sagged. He reached for the coffee. He'd done his best. His only consolation was that if Hanratty's man could find a way into this little fortress, Horn could find a way out. He murmured, "Maybe you should go after Beth. She was pretty upset. I probably shouldn't have said what I did."

McKendrick gave a disparaging sniff. "She overreacted. I know she was fond of the boy, but it is four years ago. She's a grown woman. It shouldn't still surprise her that shit happens." He buttered a slice of toast, poured himself more coffee, and only after he'd finished his breakfast did he stand up. "Help yourself, will you? I'm just going upstairs." He headed toward the hall and the massive stone staircase.

"Tell her I'm sorry," said Horn in a low voice. "For what it's worth."

"Oh, I'm not going after Beth," said McKendrick shortly. "She can come back when she's calmed down. It's time I saw to William. I won't be long."

"Who . . . ?" began Horn, but McKendrick had gone.

CHAPTER 4

H E'D HAVE GIVEN a lot for the chance to stay here, for just a few days, to catch his breath and catch up on some sleep—proper sleep, not snatched with one eye open and one ear cocked. But it wasn't an option, and he never for a moment thought it was. As soon as McKendrick's footsteps had faded on the stairs, Nicky Horn was up and through the kitchen door, looking for the way out.

He found the back door. It was locked. It wasn't like most people's back doors, locked if at all by a mortise with the key left in it. There was another keypad. The kitchen windows were also locked, sufficiently ajar to admit the air—it smelled of mown grass and wet earth—but only a fingertip.

He turned away, meaning to try his luck elsewhere, and found Beth McKendrick standing behind him. She hadn't a dagger in her hand—he checked—but there were plenty in her eyes. Horn took a step back.

"Looking for the milk?" asked Beth coldly.

"Looking for the emergency exit," admitted Horn.

She managed an icy little chuckle. "What, aren't you enjoying our hospitality? I'd have thought it would make a nice change. I don't suppose you get asked out much."

He understood her hostility, but he wasn't a patient man by nature. "Okay," he said shortly, "so we've established that you don't want me here. And I don't want to be here. If you'll open the door, I'll be on my way, and you can cheer yourself with the thought that I may be dead in a ditch before the day is out."

She made no move toward the keypad. Now he was looking at her directly rather than through the filters of shock, he could see the strong muscles in her hands and under her sleeves, the open skies in her clear blue eyes. It was a look that all climbers have, body and soul designed for strength and endurance and goals you can't achieve in an afternoon. Even if they weren't wearing crampons when they met, they recognized the look in one another and gravitated together as if drawn by magnets. Most climbers only have two kinds of friends—other climbers and paramedics.

"Patrick's father sent a hired killer after you?" She'd plaited the long chestnut hair into a thick rope to keep it out of her way. She used to wear it in pigtails, four years and a lifetime ago.

Horn nodded. "Yes."

"And *my* father brought you here. Took the risk that he'd follow you here."

"I said at the time it wasn't a great idea," growled Horn.

"Did he kidnap you? Did he force you into his car?" Horn shook his head. "So actually you could have got out and disappeared into the night," Beth pointed out. "Mack may not have known who you were and the risk he was taking by helping you, but you did. You didn't have to come back here with him. You could have thanked him for his help and said good-bye."

"I was"—he couldn't find a description that didn't sound like a plea for sympathy and finished lamely—"pretty groggy."

"Pretty groggy," she echoed, expressionless. "That's an excuse, is it? For leading a dangerous man to someone's door?"

"I didn't . . ." He heard himself starting to rise to her bait, forced his voice level again. "You're right, I shouldn't be here. Once I leave you'll be safe."

"Mack wants you to stay."

"You don't know how to open the door?"

"I didn't say that." She took the step forward that Horn had taken back, her head tipped a little to one side, exploring his face intently, as if searching for holds, for a way in. "What are you doing here?"

"I told you. Trying to leave."

"Why?"

"You know why."

"To keep us safe? That's a pretty noble gesture from anyone with a killer on his heels. From someone who dropped his best friend off a mountain when the going got tough, it's incredible." Her voice dropped a tone into cynicism. "Literally."

She seemed to want to have it all out with him again. In case there'd been some comment on his shortcomings she'd forgotten to make, some part of the old wound she'd omitted to claw open. But there was no time to indulge her; and anyway Horn knew the recriminations would just go round and round and get her nowhere. He'd ridden the carousel often enough himself.

"Beth, I can't change what happened. I can't change how you feel about me. All I can do is leave you in peace, and I can't do that unless you open the door."

"Why would I do that? I've spent the last four years wanting to meet you, working out what I'd say."

"And now you've said it. So let me go."

"Four years is a long time," she said quietly. "You have no idea how many nights I've lain awake thinking what I'd do, what I'd say, if I had you to myself. Oh no. I've a lot more I want to say before I open the door. And then I won't let you out. I'll throw you out."

Horn breathed heavily. It seemed to be all he could do right now. "Fine. But do it quickly."

She shook her head. "Revenge is a dish best served cold. Have some more coffee." She looked around. "Where's Mack?"

"Why do you call him that?"

She elevated an eyebrow. "You really don't know anything about us, do you? Everyone calls him that. Even in the City. I believe the prime minister calls him that."

"And that means you have to?" Horn shook his head, bemused. He'd never understood what made the upper classes tick. Until now, he'd had no reason to care.

"He likes it. Someone at the *FT* called him Mack the Knife and it stuck." She gave him a crocodile grin. "I suppose you call your father Dad. No—Da. Fewer consonants."

In the English comedy of manners, it's considered perfectly acceptable for the working class to deride the wealthy, but not the other way round. There were probably no other circumstances in which she'd have mocked his two-up, two-down accent. But she was too angry to be fair.

Horn had been called a lot worse than common. He'd never wasted much time fretting about his antecedents. "I never knew my father."

She laughed with a kind of savage delight. "You mean, you're a bastard in more ways than one."

"That's right," he said calmly. "My mother was the local bike—anyone could get on and give her a run round. And she never could read a bloody calendar—I've got three sisters and a brother. Funny thing is, though, she looked after us. She loved us. All I meant to my father was that he had to find another hooker. Even if I knew his name, why would I want to use it?"

He could have left it at that. Beth was looking chastened, almost a little ashamed, and he already knew her well enough to know that was a victory in itself. He didn't have to add, casually but with the sort of perfect timing that ensured the dart got clean under the skin, "Anyway, what do you suppose your father was doing in a red-light district at three in the morning? Advising the prostitutes on their share holdings?"

He was pretty sure he'd told her something she didn't know. Perhaps he'd told her something she didn't need to know. Her eyes widened and her jaw dropped for a moment before she regained control. "Like I'm going to believe you!"

Horn shrugged. "It's nothing to me if he spends his nights trawling the back streets of Black Country towns sixty miles from where he lives. He's not my father. At least"—he gave a sharklike grin—"I don't think he is. But if he was, I probably wouldn't look down my nose at people who owe their existence to men exactly like him."

"My father doesn't use prostitutes!" she shouted in his face. "He doesn't *need* to use prostitutes. Look at him—look at how we live. You think women don't queue up for a chance with him?"

"You explain it, then," said Horn, aware he'd found the chink in her armor but not particularly happy with the advantage it gave him. "I know what I was doing there—I was living there. I know what the man with the gun was doing there—he was looking for me. What was McKendrick doing there?"

She had no answer. She didn't know and couldn't imagine what would take him to such a place at such a time. She didn't believe it was the need for no-strings-attached sex. Not because the idea was anathema to her but because it was so wildly improbable. She wouldn't have been horrified if it turned out to be the truth, but she would have been astonished. If Robert McKendrick had wanted no-strings-attached sex, he could have got it a lot closer than sixty miles away. There were country clubs and golf clubs within five miles of the castle where they'd have drawn lots.

So it wasn't that. In Beth McKendrick's experience, things that improbable didn't happen; but sometimes it was in someone's interests to make it look as if they happened. She said slowly, the words putting themselves together and in the process shaping the unfledged notion in her head, "None of this is entirely real, is it?"

Horn barked a surprised laugh. He knew from the tightness of the skin, the still exquisite tenderness of the nerves of his teeth, that his face was swollen out of shape. "It felt pretty real. Especially the bit where I was looking down the barrel of a gun. And the bit where he rattled every tooth in my head—I don't think I imagined that."

But she was chewing her lip pensively. "Nor do I. I think that whoever set this up wanted to make it seem real. To both of you— you and Mack."

She'd lost him. "Set what up?"

"Someone wanted to bring you two together. Someone clever, and with money to spend on making it happen. That hit man—

whether he was a real one or just a good actor—wouldn't come cheap. And it was a pretty complicated scenario. There were a lot of ways it could have gone wrong, and it didn't. So it wasn't done on the spur of the moment—it was planned, carefully, even meticulously. Somebody tracked you down, and put the fear of God into you, and found a way of having Mack on the spot to save your sorry ass. Why? Whose interests are served by getting you and Mack together that couldn't be served by asking you both to lunch?"

Horn didn't think it was complicated. He thought it was very simple. "There's no plot. Tommy Hanratty's the one spending the money, but I wouldn't say he's particularly clever. He doesn't need to be. There's only one thought in his mind—to wipe me out." It wasn't a metaphor: that was exactly what Hanratty wanted. To expunge him, to strike him from the record. "Your head's full of wee sweetie mice."

Beth stared at him open-mouthed for a full three seconds before the sob came. Horn remembered, belatedly, where he'd first heard the expression—from Patrick. He supposed Beth had heard it from the same source. He felt a twinge of contrition. He hadn't meant to hurt her. Mostly, he'd been defending himself. "Sorry," he mumbled.

She pulled herself together almost physically, forcing down the grief that had choked her. She cleared her throat. "I've never heard anyone else say that."

"Me neither. I suppose it's an Irish thing." Horn took a deep breath. "Listen, I know how you feel about me. I don't blame you. I can apologize till the cows come home, but I can't bring him back. I can't make it not have happened. But I can go where you don't have to look at me. Just let me out. Let me go, and forget that I was ever here. You'll get what you want in the end. Sooner or later Hanratty'll catch up with me."

Now as she looked at him, for the first time Beth saw him as he was: not the monster of her nightmares, just a rather battered human being with strong arms and a stubborn expression, and fear behind his eyes that had dwelt there so long it seemed a part of him, something he would never be rid of. For a fleeting moment she almost found it in her to be sorry for him.

But she'd hated Nicky Horn for four years—more than four years, in fact. Even while Patrick was alive, she'd had reason to resent the friend who'd taken him places where she couldn't follow. The hatred had fed her, sustained her. The sight of his bruises, and knowing about the ones that didn't show, couldn't alter that.

But she was confused. He didn't seem to be lying about how he and McKendrick had met. But Beth didn't believe in a coincidence that outrageous: that when the past finally caught up with him, the only man both near enough and tough enough to come between Anarchy Horn and his just deserts was her father. There are over 60 million people in the British Isles, the vast majority of whom had no connection to Patrick Hanratty. McKendrick did. What he didn't have was a good reason for having been there. All she could think was that someone had lured him there—not Horn, who had nothing to gain from the meeting, nor Hanratty, who had everything to lose, but someone else. But think as she might, she couldn't begin to guess who, or why, or what possible bait he could have used to tempt a rich man to drive sixty miles and gamble his own life to save a pariah.

"Stay here," she said thickly. "I need to talk to Mack."

She wasn't going to open the back door. Horn gave in with a weary sigh. "He went upstairs to see to William. Who's William?"

"My uncle."

"I didn't know anyone else lived here."

"Now you do."

Horn frowned. He'd assumed William was a child. A grown man wouldn't need help getting up in the morning. So maybe that wasn't why McKendrick had left the room. Between the bruises the color drained from his face as if a tap had been turned. "Is *that* what's going on?" he choked, the fear flooding back. "Is that where McKendrick's gone—to call Tommy Hanratty?"

Beth blinked once, then looked away in disdain. "Don't be stupid."

But it made sense. Too much sense, more than anything else that had happened this morning. Horn's voice was stretched thin with shock. "That's it, isn't it? When he realized who I was, he guessed there was a price on my head. If he'd let events take their course he wouldn't have seen any of it, but if he brought me here and let Hanratty know where to find me . . . Dear God!—and I've been so bloody *grateful!*"

He spun on his heel, back toward the door; but his new understanding changed nothing. If he couldn't open it before, he still couldn't open it. One hand, accustomed to moving fast enough and gripping hard enough to ensure his survival, shot out and grabbed Beth McKendrick by the throat. "Open it. Now."

She gave a startled squawk; and perhaps she'd have done as he said, or perhaps she'd have spat in his eye and dared him to do his worst. There was no time for either of them to burn their boats. Robert

McKendrick came back through the sitting room. "Well, that's William comfortable . . ." His voice petered out as his eyes took in the scene.

The tableau of momentary violence had frozen, giving no clue as to when their relationship had turned physical. McKendrick looked at his daughter, all icy rebellion, and at Horn, pale, angry and afraid; and probably if he'd seen any signs of injury he would not have said, as he did, quite mildly, "Getting to know one another, I see." But it was hard to be sure.

CHAPTER 5

HORN SNATCHED HIS HAND BACK as if Beth's skin had burned him. "You have got to let me go," he insisted thickly. "Right now. You didn't have to get involved. If you'd stayed out of it, what came next wouldn't have been your fault. But bringing me here, and telling Hanratty where I am, that makes it your fault. That makes it murder."

He flashed a quick glance at Beth. "She said it was all a plot. That it was too neat to be coincidence. I thought she was imagining things. But she was right and I was wrong. I was more than wrong—I was crazy, believing that someone like you would risk all this"—his unsteady gaze swept only the kitchen but implied the castle and everything it represented—"for someone like me. But it wasn't for someone like me—it had to *be* me, didn't it? I'm worth a small fortune to you. And when you're rich, one fortune is never enough."

For a moment McKendrick said nothing. Then he said distantly, "I don't know what you're talking about." He didn't even try to make it sound like the truth.

"Please," begged Nicky Horn, "there's still time. It'll take him a while to get here. Hours, maybe. I can get a head start, if you let me go now." He would never have believed that, after living the way he had for four years, his life still meant enough to him that he was prepared to plead for it.

"Nobody's coming here. I told you that."

Horn tried to see things the way someone such as McKendrick might look at them. "I can't buy you off. I haven't got the sort of money Tommy Hanratty has. I haven't got the sort of money Tommy Hanratty's head gardener has. But I can do something for you that no one else can. I can save you from being a murderer. Even today, I can run far enough and fast enough that he won't catch me. So it won't matter that you phoned him."

"I didn't phone him."

"All right!" Horn made an explosive gesture with his hands. "All right. Beth was wrong. It was just coincidence that you happened to be walking past a back alley sixty miles from where you live at three in the morning, and nothing but old-fashioned courage that made you step in front of a gun. I believe you. Thousands wouldn't, but I'll try really hard to believe you. If you'll do something for me."

"Haven't I done enough already?"

Horn ignored that. "If you'll explain to me why you're so damned determined to keep me here. Because if it isn't for the money—if you haven't done a deal with Hanratty—you're going to die. All of you—you, Beth, William, the cat—the whole bloody family. If you made the call, the guy with the gun will be here soon to make a murderer of you. If you didn't, he may take a little longer, but he'll still get here, and after he's killed me he'll tidy up the loose ends. *All* the loose ends. All the people who might have seen, or heard, or heard about him. You, and everyone you care about. So tell me why. Why in God's name would you take that risk?"

McKendrick deliberated. Finally he said, "I want you to do something for me."

"*What?*" yelled Horn, exasperated beyond bearing. "You want me to do you a favor?"

"You think I haven't earned it?"

To judge from her expression, Beth was no less astonished by this development than Horn was. She turned a furrowed brow to the tall man beside her. "Mack? What's this about?"

He hushed her with a minimalist wave of the hand, his diamond gaze never leaving Horn's face. "Well?"

"I don't know," Horn responded bemusedly. He rubbed the side of his hand across his eyes. "I don't know anything anymore. I thought you saved my life out of simple humanity. Now you tell me it was so I can do something for you. So I'm wondering if maybe Beth got it right and somebody did plan all this. If maybe it was you."

"Don't be stupid," said McKendrick coldly. "I saw you were in trouble and I stepped in to help. I'd no idea what I was getting involved in. But since you turned out to be you, and the guy with the gun turned out to be working for Tommy Hanratty, and that upped the ante way beyond anything I expected, is it so unreasonable to ask you for something in return? If I can keep you alive, why would you refuse to do something for me?"

Beth, following the exchange like a spectator at a tennis match, gave Horn no chance to answer. Peering into her father's face, she demanded, "*Did* you phone someone?"

"I told you," he gritted. "No. Don't worry about it."

"Don't *worry* about it?" echoed Horn, recoiling from the pair of them, the girl who wore her hatred on her sleeve and the man who guarded his thoughts behind gray eyes like the steel shutters of his house. "The fact that there's a paid assassin on his way here right now? You think that's nothing to worry about?"

"Nobody's coming here," said McKendrick distantly. "Nobody'd get in if they came. And nobody gets out until I say so."

Horn gave up. "Then tell me what it is you want and let's put an end to this pantomime. What is it? Having trouble getting a window cleaner to go up the tower? You want someone who isn't scared of heights—or someone who won't be missed if he falls? I'm your man. Let's get on with it."

He was of course being facetious. But it was a measure of his complete bafflement that he wouldn't have been entirely surprised if McKendrick had handed him a bucket and a chammy leather.

McKendrick was still regarding him speculatively, as if he was weighing very carefully what was in front of him but hadn't decided yet what it was worth. Finally he said, "I don't want anything just now. But I'm going to want something. Maybe five years from now, maybe fifteen. Before you leave, I want your word that you'll come back when I need you to and do what I need you to do."

So this was it, thought Horn, his mind spinning, the point at which the bill was presented. He'd known no one acted as McKendrick had from sheer altruism—and in his admittedly limited experience, rich men were less inclined to altruism than others. It was how they became rich. McKendrick had saved Horn's sorry skin only because he had a use for it. There was a hollow feeling in the pit of his stomach, as if deep in the core of him he'd dared to hope someone had found him worth helping for his own sake. Now he knew better. He shouldn't have been disappointed but he was. Being in the gutter makes it easy for people to kick you in the face. It doesn't make it compulsory, and it doesn't make it any less painful.

"All right," he growled, trying to hide the hurt, "what is it you want me to do?"

"Promise you'll do it."

Horn raised an eyebrow. "Without knowing what it is?"

"I saved your life," McKendrick reminded him. He was looking at the younger man as a cat looks at a baby bird, half hungry and half amused. "Can you think of anything that would be too high a price?"

Horn didn't have to think for long. "I won't hurt anyone for you."

"Okay," said McKendrick slowly. Almost as if that might present a problem. "And if there's no victim? If it's a win/win situation where everyone gets what they want?"

"Give me a for instance."

McKendrick shook his head. "Give me your word."

"Not without knowing what I'm signing up for. I might be stupid, but I'm not that stupid."

McKendrick smiled haughtily. "You owe me. You owe me anything I care to ask of you."

"Then ask."

"I'm asking for your word."

"And I'm wondering what it is you want that's so obscene you daren't even name it."

McKendrick backed off with a sudden grin. As if it was a game of chess they were playing, and he could appreciate a smart move even when it put him at a disadvantage. "Fair enough. If I wanted a gofer I could hire one; if I wanted a personal favor, you'd expect me to ask my daughter. Clearly there's a downside.

"What you'll have to do isn't legal. If you're caught doing it, you could go to prison. A couple of years, maybe. Maybe not even that—you could get away with a suspended sentence. Even better, you may not be caught. You're used to staying ahead of the hunt. It wouldn't materially alter your lifestyle to be avoiding the police as well as Tommy Hanratty. I won't put Beth in that position because it would destroy hers."

Beth was still looking between the two of them as if she had no more idea what this was about than Horn had. "Mack? You think the two of us should have a quiet word on our own?"

McKendrick rejected that. "There's nothing to discuss. This doesn't concern you."

Her voice and her eyebrows climbed in tandem. "You reckon? If he's right, there's a hired killer on his way here. I could die today because you brought Anarchy Horn to Birkholmstead instead of leaving him to pay for what he did. If you think you're cutting me out of the loop on this, think again."

For the first time in minutes McKendrick dragged his gaze away from Nicky Horn's bruised and bewildered face and looked at his daughter. "Sorry, Beth, but that's exactly what I'm doing. Fate, providence, call it what you will, has presented me with an opportunity I can use—someone to do something for me that I can't do for myself and I won't ask you to do. Him serving a few years in Parkhurst is one thing. Maybe it's the best place for him. You spending a few years in Holloway is another thing entirely. This is between him and me. You don't get a say. You don't even get to know what I'm going to ask of him. You have to trust that I'm not doing it lightly, and I wouldn't be doing it at all if it wasn't the best thing for you and me both."

"When do I get to know what it is you want?" asked Horn.

"When the time comes that I need it."

"And you're willing to trust me? You're going to take my word that if I say I'll come back, and do what you want and go to prison for it, I will?"

"Yes."

"Why?"

"Because I'm not going to keep you here for anything up to fifteen years! You'd cost more to feed than a pony. I've told you what I want, Horn. I want you to acknowledge the debt you owe me and promise to repay it at a time of my choosing, even if there are consequences. A couple of years is still only a couple of years. When you get out, you'll have a lifetime that you wouldn't have had but for me."

"I don't know where I'll be in fifteen years."

"I'll find you," said McKendrick with a faint smile.

"The chances are I'll be dead."

"Then you'll be off the hook."

Horn gave an incredulous little chuckle. "That's it? I promise to come back here, if I can, at some undefined point in the future, and you let me go?"

"Exactly."

Thinking about it, Horn had to agree it was a good deal. Particularly since, if McKendrick was looking that far into the future, Horn saw little prospect that he could be called upon to keep his side of it. And whatever McKendrick wanted, word or no word, Horn could always refuse to do it. It might cost him the little honor he had left, but he'd do that rather than be forced into another ignoble act. All he had to do was promise, and he could leave here and take his troubles with him. From what he could see, the McKendricks had troubles enough of their own.

"Okay," he said at length. "I'll be your terrier. Whatever heels you need biting in five or fifteen years' time, if you can find me and if I can come, I'll bite them."

"On your life?"

"Right now that's a pretty cheap oath. But yes, on my life."

McKendrick smiled and let out a breath he seemed to have been holding for some time. "Good. Now—can we make you a packed lunch? Then I'll drive you to the station."

Horn declined the packed lunch. He wanted to leave here as soon as he could. Partly to protect the McKendricks, partly to get away from them. He collected his bags and went to stand pointedly in the front hall.

But McKendrick was as good as his word. A moment later he came through the little sitting room jangling his car keys, and his fingers danced over the keypad as if it were a small accordion. Horn heard the soft rasp of hidden bolts sliding, and McKendrick threw the heavy oak door wide. "There," he declared cheerfully, "it's going to be a lovely . . ."

And there he stopped. His tall, spare frame froze rigid on the top step, his steel-gray eyes lancing across the surrounding gardens to the dark line of high hedges beyond. "What the hell . . . ?"

Horn, all alertness and dread, was beside him in a moment; even so he was too late. He looked where McKendrick was looking but saw nothing. "What?"

"There's someone down there," said Robert McKendrick, and the indignation in his voice was barred with an unmistakable note of shock.

CHAPTER 6

IT MIGHT HAVE BEEN a trick, a strategy to keep him there. Horn didn't think so, for two reasons. One was that stunned note in McKendrick's voice. The other was that he went on standing there, staring at the distant hedge, framed in the doorway like an assassin's birthday present, long after anyone who'd been even half expecting this would have dived back inside.

"McKendrick! *McKendrick!*" But he seemed not to hear until Horn grabbed the back of his jacket and hauled him bodily inside. "Lock it down. Now!"

The sound of the lockdown that had startled her from sleep two hours earlier now brought Beth hurrying into the hall. "*Now* what?"

"I saw someone."

"Who?"

"*I* don't know!"

"I do," said Horn grimly. "I knew this was taking too damn long."

"You mean . . . ?" As if McKendrick hadn't taken seriously

anything Horn had said until now. "It's not possible. No one could have followed us here."

"He's followed me everywhere else."

McKendrick shook his head. "He wasn't behind us on the road. I'll swear to it."

"I don't know how he does it. I don't know how they perform brain surgery either. It's what he does for a living, and he's good at it. Tommy Hanratty wouldn't employ him if he wasn't."

"Perhaps it was Childs," said Beth.

Horn didn't believe these people. It was as if nothing that had happened, nothing that had been said, had struck them as important enough to remember. As if, with the deck chairs floating off around them, they were still telling one another that the *Titanic* couldn't sink. He gritted his teeth. "Who's Childs?"

"The local vicar. He's a bit of a twitcher. He comes up here bird-watching sometimes," said McKendrick.

Horn was working hard at not screaming. "You have to listen to me. Your lives depend on it. That isn't a vicar wandering around looking for godwits, it's a hired killer. I know it's a lot to take in. But *you* know he isn't a figment of my imagination—you've seen him, spoken to him. You've seen his gun."

McKendrick gave a reluctant nod.

"I told you he was coming, and now he's here. Do you remember what else I said? That when he left, he'd leave no one alive to talk about it. *Now* do you believe me?"

Neither of them answered him. But he felt the air about them shiver with their thinking.

"Get the police," said Horn. "It's too late for anything else. But for pity's sake, warn them what they're up against. They need to come armed and mob-handed. He'll kill anyone who gets in his way."

After a long moment McKendrick turned to his daughter. "Do it. We can explain later. Use the landline, I don't think we've time to be hunting for a mobile signal."

Finally, thought Horn. *Finally* the man realizes he's put his own life and his daughter's life and even his brother William's life in danger. Maybe now I can get some sense out of him.

Still for a moment Beth hesitated. But then she nodded, and turned and ran across the hall, back into the sitting room.

"How long will it take them to get here?"

McKendrick shrugged. "Our nearest police station is about twenty minutes away. I don't know if they're equipped to deal with a professional assassin."

Horn looked at the windows, steel-shuttered again and admitting no light. When he'd installed the castle's latest defenses, McKendrick had known that one day his life might depend on them. He'd spared no expense. "Okay. Well, these shutters should keep him out for longer than that."

The tall man looked indignant. "These shutters should keep him out, full stop! Have you any idea what they cost?"

Horn neither knew nor cared. "Nothing will keep him out forever. Men like him found ways across the Iron Curtain at the height of the Cold War. If armies and mines couldn't beat them, a bit of steel shuttering won't either. But it will slow him down. The cavalry should get here before he finds the weak spot."

"There is no weak spot."

"There's always a weak spot. Give him time to feel his way round, look at what you've got and what you haven't, work out where you compromised because of the Grade II listing, and he'll be walking round in here like he owns the place. But time's on our side. All we have to do is make sure he can't get inside in the next twenty minutes.

"One thing," Horn added. "You'd better warn your brother, and get him down here. We should all be together."

McKendrick blinked stupidly at him. "My brother?"

Horn rolled his eyes. "Your brother William. He doesn't know what's going on, does he? And if we're not all together, we can't be sure who's making any noises we hear."

McKendrick pursed his lips. "You're quite good at this, aren't you?"

"I've *got* good at it," growled Horn. "Now—William?"

"Problem with that," said McKendrick pensively. "William has to stay in his room."

Horn stared at him in disbelief. "What—use the wrong knife for his fish, did he? Punish him another time. Right now he needs to come down here."

McKendrick regarded him with dislike. "William's an invalid. He can't leave his room."

"Oh, for . . . !" But there wasn't time to waste talking about it. "Okay. These shutters—they cover his windows as well?"

"Well, no," admitted McKendrick. "I was advised that securing the first three floors was all that was necessary—that no one could mount a serious attack any higher than that. William's room is on the next floor up. For the view."

Momentarily distracted, Horn looked puzzled. "Who did you upset? I know who's trying to kill me, and why. But why does someone like you need this level of security?"

McKendrick raised a haughty eyebrow at him. "Money, of course. I told you. It's not just my personal fortune, I control assets equal to the gross national product of quite a large country. That makes me a target for anyone with more muscle than morals. I consulted a security expert and he said the biggest danger I faced was kidnapping. Not so much me as Beth—that someone could snatch her and hold her to ransom."

Privately, Horn thought that anyone who snatched Beth McKendrick would send her back pretty quickly and might pay a small premium to complete the deal. He thought about the shutters and the keypads, and the bank of monitors in the entrance hall, and sniffed. "It might have been cheaper to pay the ransom."

McKendrick shook his head decisively. "You don't pay ransom. Ever. If you do, it's going to happen again."

And the really scary thing was, Horn believed him. It wasn't just lip service that would collapse as soon as it was put under any pressure. This rich, important and powerful man had supplemented his stone walls with steel shutters because he didn't want to lose his daughter, not because he didn't want to lose his money.

Horn gave himself a mental shake. McKendrick's priorities weren't the issue right now. "Those screens in the hall—that's the CCTV?" McKendrick nodded. "Then the rest of us stay there and watch. Of course, he'll have located the cameras by now. But we might get a bit of warning when he's ready to make his play."

Four monitors were grouped around a console behind the exercise bike. Currently they were showing four entirely static views of the McKendrick estate. In one a couple of sheep were grazing in the middle distance; none of the others showed a living soul.

Horn thought there'd be more channels but he couldn't work

out how to access them. Joiners don't spend that much computer time. Recognizing his difficulty, McKendrick took over. "What do you want to see?"

"Everything. How many cameras are there?"

"Sixteen." McKendrick tapped keys crisply, and each of the four screens divided itself into four. "They cover all the approaches, all the doors, the courtyard, the front terrace and the gardens."

Horn leaned closer to the monitors, watching for movement. But there was nothing.

Then there was. Not a movement, but suddenly one corner of one screen went blank. McKendrick frowned and tapped the glass repeatedly. "Malfunc—?" Before he'd even finished the word he realized how stupid it would sound. "Probably not."

"Where's that camera?" asked Horn quietly. His absolute focus gave McKendrick a glimpse of how someone whose idea of fun was playing Russian roulette with a mountaintop dealt with stress. By moving onto a separate level where there's no room for panic because doing the right things in the right order is what keeps death at bay. A man whose mind worked like that could believe he was capable of anything.

"At the gateway into the courtyard," said McKendrick. "That's where he is."

Horn shook his head. "That's where he was twenty seconds ago. He'll be somewhere else now."

"Why didn't we see him?"

"Because he doesn't want to be seen." McKendrick might be playing catch-up with the crisis, but at least Horn no longer suspected him of orchestrating it. He'd been genuinely taken aback by the turn events had taken. No one is that good an actor. McKendrick had thought they couldn't be found right up to the moment that they were, and possibly a little longer.

Horn had known they could be found, and would be found, and the only question was how quickly. He wasn't shocked at the development. He was sickened to find himself doing this again so soon. And he was tired, tired to the marrow of his bones, with running and running and only taking his problems with him. And he felt guilty that someone who'd tried to help him, whatever his reasons, however selfish his motives, was going to pay a price he could never have guessed for his intervention. Horn hadn't sought his help, had tried to warn him what it would mean, had tried to be somewhere else when the pursuit caught up with him. None of this stopped him from feeling like a murderer.

"You think I'm good at this? I'm an amateur. The guy out there's the professional. He does it again and again, and he always wins in the end. He wouldn't stay in business if he didn't."

"But . . ." McKendrick was still struggling with the evidence of his eyes. "This isn't right . . ."

Horn barked a grim little laugh. "Well, no. I guess contract killings *are* frowned on in polite society. I wouldn't know—more to the point, neither would Tommy Hanratty. He thinks it's right enough if it's what he wants."

Movement behind them made both of them start. But it was Beth. Her face was expressionless but her voice was as taut as a steel hawser. "The landline's dead."

McKendrick sucked in a sharp breath. Horn gave a shrug that was a brave attempt at fatalism. "He's cut it. Of course he has."

"And the mobiles?" asked McKendrick.

"Couldn't get a signal on either of them. But there's nothing unusual about that."

Horn stared at her. "You have mobile phones that can't get a signal?"

"At home we use the landline," she retorted. "Or walk as far as the ha-ha." She offered him her phone. "Give it a try."

"Ha ha," said Horn coldly, and it might have been a question or a comment, but he didn't take up her invitation.

There was half a minute's silence while they all considered the situation. McKendrick broke it. "So, essentially, we can't get help, we can't tell anybody we're in trouble, you don't reckon the vastly expensive security system I installed will keep him out forever, and you reckon that when he gets in he'll kill us all. Is that a fair assessment?"

The shock was dissipating. Horn was impressed by McKendrick's businesslike tone. "Pretty much." Something occurred to him. "With all these shutters and things, didn't you get one of those alarms that ring in the nearest police station?"

McKendrick had the grace to look embarrassed. "Well, yes and no. I installed one. It went off so often when it wasn't meant to that they said they wouldn't answer it anymore."

Horn's expression froze on his face. "So twenty minutes away there's a policeman looking at a flashing light saying, 'Not them again!' and sending out for a cup of tea?"

"'Fraid so."

Beth was eyeing her father with a mixture of exasperation and almost enough affection to eclipse the fear. "Go on—tell him the rest."

McKendrick dropped his eyes and mumbled something.

"Sorry?"

76

"I said," he repeated forcefully, "I kept playing with it! All right? This is my fault. You can die with a clear conscience, and Beth with a satisfied smile, because this is all my fault. Or, and this is just a thought, we can try to find some way of not dying, at least not yet. What do you think?"

"I know a way of not dying," said Beth softly. "For most of us, anyway."

Horn had a fair idea what was coming. McKendrick seemed not to. "Let's hear it."

She nodded at Horn. "If Mr. Hanratty's man gets what he came for, he'll go away."

Neither of them looked at the visitor. They looked at one another, the cool, narrow man and the strong, passionate woman, father and daughter with so much in common and so much not, chips cut off opposite facets of the same block. McKendrick blinked first. "I'm not going to open the door and shove him outside!"

"You won't have to. Not if he volunteers."

Her father's voice soared. "Do you know what you're asking?"

Beth gave a disingenuous shrug. "He's been begging you to let him out of here. Do as he asks."

"That was before"—her father jerked a nod at the bank of monitors—"turned up. When he thought he had a head start."

"So now it's a short head. Maybe he can still get away. He said it himself, he's been doing this long enough to get good at it. He has a better chance out there than either of us. If he gets through, he can send help."

"He won't get through."

"He might."

"He won't."

Finally Beth looked at the subject of their discussion. Her eyes were cold and her voice unyielding. "Then better him than us. He should have died four years ago, trying to save Patrick. He bottled it. Now he gets another chance. He can die saving us instead."

When Horn at last found a voice, it seemed to come from a lot farther away than the pit of his stomach. "You know, don't you, that it won't change anything? After he's killed me, he'll come in here and kill you."

Her smile was more than half a sneer, then she looked back at McKendrick. "It's just another lie. He's trying to hide behind us. Why would anybody risk hanging around after he'd committed a murder?"

"Because you've seen his face." Horn too was speaking directly to McKendrick. He knew that if his fate depended on persuading Beth, he was already a dead man. "He won't leave any witnesses."

"But . . ." McKendrick stopped, swallowed, started again, his voice cranked down to a normal, rational tone. "Look, Beth, maybe he's mistaken. Pro or not, maybe the shutters *will* keep him out. He knows Horn won't be here forever. When he leaves, he'll pick up the trail again and corner him somewhere he'll be easier to deal with. Where there won't *be* any witnesses."

"You're missing the point," growled Horn. "You're already a danger to him—you were the moment you decided to step into that alleyway instead of walking past. You've seen him, talked to him. He knows you know what he is. You don't have to see him kill me to be a witness against him. This man's livelihood, his whole way of life, depends on him not having a face. You've seen his face."

Horn turned to Beth, and his expression was stony but there was regret in his eyes. "I'll tell you something else. If I take my chances out there, and somehow manage to get past him, he won't follow me. Right now McKendrick is more of a threat to him than I can ever be. He can always find me again. But if he leaves here now, he knows what'll happen. McKendrick'll go to the police. He'll sit down with a PhotoFit guy and come up with a likeness that'll go out to every police station, railway station, airport and dock in England, and across the Channel to Interpol. He'll never be able to work again. Finally he'll be picked up as the result of a minor traffic accident in Marseille or somewhere. *That's* why he has to kill you. All of you. If it'll make him safer, even just a little bit safer, he won't hesitate."

Beth's jaw was clamped so tight she had to force the words out. "Don't believe him. He'd say anything, do anything, to save his precious skin."

Horn managed a cynical laugh. "Unlike you, of course, willing to lay down your life to do what's right."

"This *is* right," she sneered.

McKendrick sighed. "Beth, I know how you feel about him. But you can't kill a man for doing something that upset you. You lost a good friend on Anarchy Ridge; but it wasn't Horn's fault. Maybe he could have acted differently. Maybe you would have acted differently. Or maybe you just think you would. I don't know. I don't know what I'd have done in the same circumstances.

"I do know that the authorities both in Alaska and back here in England looked at the facts and decided he didn't have a case to answer. That Patrick Hanratty's death wasn't murder, or even manslaughter, but misadventure. Those boys were up there doing something they loved, and it went wrong and only one of them came back. It happened to be Horn; it could as easily have been Patrick. The mountains take a tithe. It was their turn to pay, that's all."

He turned to Horn, was startled to see a brilliance in his eye that looked for a moment like tears. McKendrick cleared his throat. "Just so we're not making any assumptions, would you sooner take your chances out there alone or in here with us?"

It took Horn a few seconds to answer. McKendrick hadn't imagined the tears—they'd welled in sheer gratitude that finally someone understood. Horn had never hoped for forgiveness, that would be too much, but dear God he'd ached for a gram of human understanding. His voice was gruff, to disguise what he believed was a weakness. "I doubt it'll make much difference. Not in the long term. Probably not in the short term either."

"All the more reason," McKendrick insisted, "that you get a say in how we do this."

Horn hadn't expected to be consulted. It was a long time since anyone had put much value on either his life or his opinions. He wasn't sure what to say. "If you think—if Beth thinks—you'll have a better chance if we split up, I'll make a run for it."

"That's not what I asked."

"No." Still he hesitated. "Okay. Then, I don't know how long your shutters will keep out bullets, but they'll do it for longer than my skin will. If I get a choice, I'll stay here."

"Fine. Good," said McKendrick.

Beth stared at him as if he'd given away her birthright—which perhaps, in a way, he had. "You'd protect him? You'd put our lives on the line to protect *him*?"

McKendrick nodded. "I brought him here. What happens now is my responsibility. I'm not throwing him to the wolves as the price of our safety. For one thing, I think he's right—I doubt it would work."

"Let's try it and find out."

"No. Sorry, Beth, but when it comes right down to it, this is my house and I'll extend whatever protection it can offer to whoever I choose. If I'm going to die today, I don't want to go trying to appease a hired killer. I've made plenty of mistakes in my life, but I don't think I've done much to be ashamed of. That changes if I open the front door and push Horn through it. Even if he's wrong and you're right, and we could save ourselves that way, it's too high a price. I'm sorry."

If it had been someone else—anyone else—she'd probably have agreed with him. She was a strong and determined woman, who'd faced the prospect of death and the idea that there are things worth dying for when she first started climbing. No one needs to risk their neck on the snow and ice and crumbling rotten rock of a mountain ascent. They do it because the emotional payback of success is worth the possibility of disaster.

McKendrick believed with all his heart that if it had been just the family here, or if they'd found themselves protecting some luckless fugitive whose life and struggles she knew nothing about, his daughter would have applied herself to the task with a courage and dignity that would have made him proud. That it was only her hatred of Horn, that soul-consuming passion she could see neither through nor past, that made her think that buying her life with his was a bargain.

"What the hell are you thinking?" she yelled, the chestnut braid flying in her rage. "Maybe you have the right to risk your own life, however worthless the prize—but it isn't just your life you're risking, is it? I'm your daughter—Uncle William's your brother. And you're prepared to sacrifice us all, and for what? *That?* That abject apology for a man? A deadweight who cut his best friend's rope when the going got tough?"

"Beth," said McKendrick softly, "can't you see that you're proposing to do exactly the same thing? To cut Horn loose because trying to save him will put us in danger? At least Horn and Patrick were friends, and they were up on Anarchy Ridge because they couldn't think of anywhere they'd rather be. Can't you see, it would be so much worse to do it to someone you didn't care about? Someone who never chose to put his life in your hands?"

The comparison hurt her womb-deep. The mere mention of her lost friend's name brought bitter tears to her eyes and her voice. "I don't know how you can say that to me."

"Because we're up against the wall here," said McKendrick apologetically. "It's my fault and I'm sorry. If I could go back and do it differently, I would. I never thought for a moment that what I was doing could have any implications for you. You must believe that. I would never willingly put you in danger. You matter more to me than anything. I hoped one day you'd understand that, but if we're running out of *one days* . . ."

He stopped and swallowed, then went on. "If we're running out of *one days* it's important that we do this right. We'll only get one chance. If we make a bad decision now, it won't be a question of living with it but it will be what posterity remembers us by. Do you believe there's a hired killer out there?"

"Yes!" she said hotly. "Like I've been trying to tell you! Like *Horn* has been trying to tell you."

"A professional. A man hired by Tommy Hanratty to avenge the death of his son."

"Exactly."

"Then do you honestly believe that, having killed Horn, he'll drive away and leave us alone?"

She stood her ground. "Yes."

McKendrick stooped a little to peer into her eyes. "Honestly?"

"Yes," she repeated firmly. "A professional won't kill anyone he doesn't have to, because every hit increases the danger to himself and the risk of exposure to his employer."

"Horn thinks he'll kill us to protect himself and Hanratty."

"But then"—her lip curled—"he would think that, wouldn't he?"

McKendrick gave an oddly gentle little sigh. "He's offered to try and make a run for it. If you're right, I should take that offer. If *he's* right, I shouldn't."

Beth shrugged, her strong, limber body stiff with resentment. "What's the alternative? Waiting till we starve to death? Drawing lots for who we eat first?"

"That's pretty much how castle sieges used to end," agreed McKendrick ruefully. "Either the guys inside got hungry and came out, or the guys outside got hungry and went away."

"Is anybody going to come looking for you?" Horn wasn't sure if he was helping his own cause or not.

"In a few days, maybe. Not before."

"Even when they can't get you on the phone?"

"Like I say—in a few days."

Horn scowled. "I thought you big international businessmen had to keep in touch? That the economy would collapse if you didn't?"

McKendrick gave a small smile. "A myth put about by us big international businessmen, to justify our absurd salaries."

"So we're on our own?" Horn shook his head and shut his eyes to conceal the despair. "It won't take him days to find a way in."

"Castles like this held out for months," objected McKendrick, though he didn't sound altogether convinced.

"At a time when gunpowder and the armour-piercing bodkin were cutting-edge technology," said Horn dismissively. "The guy out there will have access to plastic explosive, shaped charges, rocket-propelled grenades, the lot. A tin-pot little toy castle? Given a couple of hours, he could muster enough firepower to take over a city."

It was time for a decision, and McKendrick made it. "Well, actually the choice isn't that difficult. If you're right we're all going to die whatever we do. There's no need to make it easy for him, or throw away the outside chance that we can hold him off long enough for something to change. And if Beth's right and he's only interested in killing you, we don't have to make a choice now—only if he gets in here. We'll batten down the hatches and wait to see what happens."

Beth opened her mouth to argue but McKendrick stilled her with a hard look. "I know—you'd do it differently. But this is my house, and the responsibility is mine. I'm sorry if it turns out to be a bad call.

"So let's come up with some ideas to improve the odds. Make it harder for him. Keep him out for longer, prepare a plan of action for if he gets inside. Birkholmstead is still a stone-built fortification—even if he gets in, we can retreat from room to room and keep him at bay for hours, maybe days. In the meantime, we'll keep checking the mobiles—we only have to get a signal on one of them for five minutes and we can end this."

She still didn't like it, but finally Beth accepted that it wasn't a battle she could win. "I'll do the phones. I'll take them up on the roof every ten minutes or so—if there's a signal going, that's where we'll get it."

"Make sure he doesn't see you," warned Horn. "With a good sniper rifle he could be accurate to as much as a mile."

"I won't stay still long enough for him to use it."

"Do you have a flagpole?" asked Horn.

McKendrick looked puzzled. "On top of the tower."

"Then we can fly a distress signal."

"This isn't a ship of the line!" snorted Beth. "We have a Union Jack, not a wardrobe of pennants! We can't send England Expects and all that stuff."

"We can fly the Union Jack upside down," said McKendrick. "The universal distress signal."

Trying to picture it, Horn frowned. "Doesn't it look pretty much the same both ways up?"

"Pretty much," admitted McKendrick. "It would take an expert to notice, even from close up."

"And anyone who gets that close probably won't get to leave," said Horn grimly. "I don't think we should count on anyone noticing which way up the flag is."

"Then we'll fly a tablecloth instead," said McKendrick, suddenly inspired. "The biggest, whitest one I can find. Flag of truce. *That* would be noticed, even from a distance. Whoever saw it might not know what it meant, but he'd know it meant *something*."

"Would he know to call the police rather than come blundering up to the front door to ask what the problem is?" wondered Beth. "Come to that, would the police know to send a SWAT team, or would we get a couple of PCs on their way back from liaising with a Neighborhood Watch scheme?"

McKendrick looked as if she'd slapped his face. But it was a point. He didn't want to see a couple of twenty-something constables mown down investigating a bit of table linen on a stick.

"I think," said Horn, "he won't pick a fight with the police unless he's cornered. Because he knows that, the world over, there are two kinds of murder hunts—those where the victim was a civilian, and those where he was a police officer. They pull out every stop in the organ when it was a cop who got killed. Of course they do—it's personal. It also means they're dealing with someone who'll stop at nothing. No professional hit man wants to be the subject of that kind of manhunt. I think, if he sees a police car coming and he has the chance to slip away, that's what he'll do."

"All right," decided McKendrick. "We'll hoist a tablecloth and try to attract attention. Beth will keep trying the phones. Next we need a line of retreat . . ."

Beth touched his arm. "No, next you should check on Uncle William. Will you tell him what's going on?"

McKendrick shook his head. "No point upsetting him when there's nothing he can do to help. But I will draw the curtains."

Horn shook his head. "Don't do anything to mark out his room as different. You draw his curtains, the guy outside knows there's something in there you want to protect." He hesitated. "Look, I don't want to be insensitive, but what's the problem with your brother William? Why can't we bring him down here with us?"

For a moment he thought McKendrick wasn't going to answer. "Beth, where's that damask tablecloth your mother used to use for dinner parties? Oh, yes—I know. Horn, you come with me. When we've got it flying, I'll take you in to meet William. You can see for yourself what the problem is."

CHAPTER 7

FROM THE top of the tower Horn had a panoramic view of the heart of England. It was very green, and rather flat, and populated by trees and hedgerows and not so many people. In fact, none that he could see. Not only no people but no signs of people, unless you knew that the straight lines carved through the fields were the mark of tractors. There were no dwellings in sight. He could see no roads other than the driveway by which they had arrived.

From this vantage he could see Birkholmstead more or less as a plan on a map, and it gave him a better impression of the castle than he'd managed from inside. It really wasn't very big. There would be comfortable stockbroker Tudor houses in any leafy suburb that covered as much ground, though none would have matched it for height. The tower was the highest point, but it was only the size of one fairly small room—the attic room the spiraling steps had brought them through—with a crenellated parapet through whose slits an earlier generation of defenders had ranged their arrows.

The tower was not central but offset to one side so that looking down he could see the leads of another roof, and below it again a wider one that had been turned into a terrace by the addition of a couple of bistro chairs and a table. The main entrance where McKendrick had left his car was on the south side, and there was another in the stone-flagged courtyard to the west, which Horn supposed was Beth's. He walked round the high parapet, looking for a third, and couldn't spot it.

And then he did. A dark green station wagon was drawn up against the boundary hedge a quarter of a mile away, all but invisible to anyone who hadn't a really good reason for looking, totally un-memorable to anyone lacking a really good reason to remember. Horn had such a reason. And that wasn't the car he'd been forced into six hours earlier. The first thing Hanratty's man had done after McKendrick interrupted him at his work was change his car. The con-summate professional. The thought cheered Nicky Horn not at all.

McKendrick was attaching his mother-in-law's best supper cloth to the flag halyard with deft movements of his wrists and knots that Horn didn't recognize. Of course, when Horn tied a knot he was about to trust his life to it, not a nice bit of table linen. "Do this a lot, do you?"

McKendrick grinned. "Not as much as I do it on the boat."

Horn nodded toward the distant car. "I'm guessing that doesn't belong to the bird-watching vicar."

McKendrick peered where he was indicating. "You think that's our friend's?"

Horn strove to remain polite. "I'm pretty sure it will be."

"I still don't know how the hell he got here."

"He followed us. He just did it carefully."

But McKendrick wouldn't have it. "I'd have known. It's a two-hour drive, and a lot of it's on roads that no one else uses, at least not in the early hours of the morning. He couldn't have kept us in sight without me seeing him, at least from time to time. I'm telling you, there was no one behind us."

To Horn the answer was obvious. "There must have been. Unless you really did call him when we got here."

McKendrick bent on him a look of disfavor, declining to dignify the accusation with a reply. He peered at the distant car. "Can you see him?"

"I don't expect to. Not till it's too late."

McKendrick frowned at him. "You're a pessimistic son of a bitch, aren't you?"

"I'm a realist."

McKendrick considered for a moment. "You climb, I sail. We've both been in more life-threatening situations than most people. We've both walked away from situations that could have killed us— that *should* have killed us. What's to say this won't be another one?"

"The sea isn't trying to kill you," Horn reminded him, tight-lipped. "The mountains don't care if you live or die. Him out there: he cares. He cares enough to keep trying until he succeeds. He won't give up. He'll keep coming back till he finishes the job."

"Believe that and you're as good as dead already."

"I know," said Horn, and it was in his eyes and in his voice that while he'd long ago reached the same conclusion, he had never come to terms with it. "Mr. McKendrick, I've been a dead man running since Tommy Hanratty realized the law wasn't going to give him the satisfaction he required. At first it was his own people, heavies off his payroll. It wasn't too hard staying ahead of them. They're not the sharpest knives in the drawer—most of them could be out-thought by a rubber duck. When Hanratty realized that as well, he got in a pro. And he's a whole different ball game. I'm still running. But I know I can't stay ahead of him forever."

McKendrick regarded him thoughtfully. "Call me Mack."

Somehow, that wasn't what Horn was expecting. "What?"

"Everyone calls me Mack. Even Beth. If we're going to die together, we might as well be on first-name terms."

"Fine. Whatever." It really wasn't Horn's highest priority just now. "You can call me . . ."

"Yes?" A small waiting smile.

"*Anything* but Anarchy Horn."

They went back inside, down one flight of narrow stairs onto a corridor, stopped at a black oak door. "This is William's room." But McKendrick didn't knock before they went in.

Invalids' rooms, whether in castles or cottages, have only two smells. Well-cared-for invalids smell of talcum powder; neglected invalids smell of urine. William McKendrick's room smelled of talcum powder.

It was a big room, and because it occupied one corner of the castle its mullioned windows commanded views on two sides. Under one was a comfortable sofa with a coffee table and a scattering of magazines. The second had been converted to French windows that opened onto the little terrace Horn had seen from the tower. Inside the door to the left was a large oak armoire, to the right a chest of drawers with a television on top of it, at the foot of the bed a big carved blanket-box. It was a high bed, higher than normal, and not Jacobean oak but painted metal festooned with power lines. A hospital bed. It had been positioned close to the French windows, for the air and the view.

As he looked, at first Horn thought the bed was empty. The

sheets seemed too flat to conceal a human being. Nevertheless, that was where William McKendrick was: in his high hospital bed, sitting up against his starched white pillows, gazing out of his French window with the distant preoccupation that the very clever sometimes share with the almost vegetative.

For another moment Horn wasn't sure which camp the other McKendrick belonged in. Then Mack left Horn's side and, taking a tissue, wiped a strand of drool from his brother's perfectly shaven jaw. He said softly, "This is my brother William. Someone to see you, Billy."

Horn hesitated in the doorway, feeling awkward. "Won't he mind . . . ?"

Robert McKendrick smiled and shook his head. "William likes visitors. His social circle isn't what it once was. I'm sure he's bored to death seeing the same old faces all the time."

William McKendrick's eyes were a pale and faded blue, and Horn was not convinced that they saw anything at all. Or, if they saw, that his brain made any sense of the image. He looked at Horn with the same uncritical incomprehension that Horn had once looked at a painting by Picasso.

Horn swallowed. "Was it a stroke?"

Mack shook his head again. "Alzheimer's disease. Senile dementia."

"He doesn't look old enough."

"He was unlucky," said McKendrick distantly. "It started while he was in his early fifties. The peak of his career. He was a barrister." He smiled at the man in the bed, who smiled back hesitantly as if wondering if that was the expected response. "The terror of the Old Bailey, weren't you, Billy? Horace Rumpole had nothing on you. And then this started."

Horn wasn't sure how much he was expected to contribute. "How old is William now?"

"He's sixty-two. He's ten years older than I am."

"And how long . . . ?" Horn didn't finish the sentence, aware that it verged on the impertinent.

"Has he been like this? Completely locked in, about three years. But he's been ill for nearly ten, and every one of those years took away more of his past and his personality. It's a cruel disease, Nicky. Most illnesses can only threaten your present and your future. Dementia steals both the past and the person who lived it."

"I'm sorry," said Horn, though he was aware it didn't go far. He looked again at the man in the bed, trying to fathom how much of him was left. "Does he understand what we're saying?" He meant, Should we be talking in front of him?

"I'm not sure," said McKendrick honestly. "There's a lot that passes him by. On the other hand, he knows where he is—if we have to move him he becomes terribly distressed. I stopped taking him for hospital appointments. They weren't doing him any good, and being in a strange place upset him. So now we do what we can for him here, and what we can't do doesn't get done."

"You look after him?" Even with all the equipment, it was hard to overestimate the scale of the commitment.

"He has a nurse who comes in by day." McKendrick saw Horn's eyes widen, anticipated his next question. "Usually. I gave him the week off. I knew I was going to be around, it seemed a good chance." He lifted narrow shoulders in a rueful shrug. "Not necessarily the best call ever. Except, of course, from the nurse's point of view."

Horn nodded slowly. "And that's it, is it? That's everyone in the house? No more surprises? William doesn't have a wife and six children that you haven't got round to mentioning yet?"

"William *does* have a wife," said McKendrick, "and two children. Margot lives in the States; I don't know where the kids are now. They couldn't cope with William's illness. They were used to depending on him, couldn't face the idea that he was going to be dependent on them. For everything, for the rest of his life."

"She left him?" It was none of his business, and Horn tried to keep his voice neutral.

McKendrick gave a gruff chuckle. "Not exactly. She just went on holiday and hasn't come back yet."

"When?"

"About eight years ago."

Horn's family had never been the conventional nuclear model, but it had been warm and close and he'd been into his teens before he realized it was unusual enough to raise eyebrows. But he'd cut himself off from them after Alaska. Not because they blamed him for what happened. All the Horns were fiercely loyal: matriarch Angela, she of the Velcro-fastened underwear, took as her mantra the Arab proverb "Me and my brother against my cousin, me and my cousin against the world." They'd have stood shoulder to shoulder with Nicky whatever he'd done: it was how they operated. It was his decision to stay away. If a man with a gun came to their door one day, he wanted them to be able to say with absolute honesty that they hadn't heard from Nicky in years. Not because he thought they might betray him, but because he was genuinely afraid what Tommy Hanratty might do if he thought they could provide the information he wanted and wouldn't.

But he never stopped loving them and he never stopped missing them. Two of his sisters had families of their own now: he was an uncle. His mother had been starting to have trouble with her eyes. It weighed on him that she might be blind by now and he didn't know. Sometimes he spent all night plotting how he might get in touch with one or another of them without leaving a trail; but in the cold, hard light of morning he always decided it simply wasn't worth the risk. For himself he'd have taken it, but not for them. They had so much more to lose.

So while to all intents and purposes he had no family now, it wasn't long since he'd been an integral part of a close-knit clan whose members argued passionately and behaved irresponsibly and loved without reservation. And he couldn't imagine any one of them turning their backs on another of them who fell ill.

McKendrick saw him recoil and his tone softened. "It's asking a lot, you know. William now isn't the man that she married. You expect to grow old and stiff and doddery together—you don't expect that one of you will jump the gun by thirty years. It sounds great, doesn't it—all that *in sickness and in health* stuff. And if he'd fallen off his hunter and ended up in a wheelchair, or if he'd got cancer and gone bald and frail and left her a widow before she was fifty, I don't doubt she'd have done her best for him and seen it through to the bitter end. Alzheimer's is different. It doesn't kill you. William could live into his nineties. But everything that made him William— that made Margot marry him and have two children with him—has gone. I never held it against her—well, not really, not for long—that she didn't want to see him reduced like this." He gave his brother a friendly grin that robbed the words of their sting.

"Marriage is a matter of choice," he went on pensively. "You choose someone to spend your life with. If they change, even if it's not their fault, maybe it's fair enough to consider all bets off. The family you're born into is different. They *have* to take you as you are, for better or worse. If Margot finally gets a divorce, William will no longer be her husband. But he'll always be my brother." He looked at the man in the bed with a mixture of sorrow and affection. "I promised him this would be his home for as long as he lived."

A terrible thought occurred to McKendrick. "My God. You don't suppose he"—a glance toward the window and the car at the bottom of the garden—"would kill the rest of us and leave William alive?"

It was possible. Even a very cautious man could see no danger of being identified by William McKendrick. But it was plain, in Mack's face and in his tone, that that was not the reassurance he sought. Horn told him what he needed to hear. "No. By the time he gets in here, he'll just want to finish the job as quickly as he can and get out again. He won't even ask himself why William's still in bed."

The tall man nodded, relieved. He said in a low voice, "I'd kill him myself before I'd let that happen. Before I'd leave him to be nursed in a geriatric ward."

Horn believed him. He cleared his throat, changed the subject. "So if we can't move William downstairs, how are we going to do this?"

"I'll stay here. We won't make any noise, will we, Billy? You watch the monitors in the hall."

"I don't know how to operate the security system."

"Beth does."

Horn had no wish to spend the last few hours of his life with someone who despised him. "Or Beth could sit with William."

"She can't lift him on her own. I can. Except . . ." McKendrick looked at the bedside table, indicated a plastic device with an incongruous clown's face. "There's the baby monitor. We can keep the speaker with us. Then if she needs a hand, she can let me know." His voice adopted the bright, cheery tone appropriate for addressing invalids. "That all right, Billy? If Beth comes and sits with you for a while?" There was no measurable alteration in the white-faced basilisk stare. "Good. Fine."

McKendrick headed back downstairs, Horn in his wake. All he could see of McKendrick was his back disappearing round the central column of the spiral stairway. It encouraged a kind of intimacy. He murmured, "I'm sorry about your brother."

A shade unexpectedly, McKendrick stopped, pivoted on one heel, and looked back and upward, his gray eyes searching. "Thank you."

"I'm sorry for all of this."

"It's not your fault."

"No, I don't think it is. But you wouldn't be in danger if you hadn't stopped to help me."

McKendrick thought for a moment. "I knew what I was doing. That there could be consequences. I never thought there could be consequences for Beth, but that isn't your fault either."

Horn sucked in a deep breath. "I meant what I said. If you think it'll do any good—if you think it *might* do some good—I'll go out and meet him. Let what happens happen."

McKendrick was still regarding him with that pale, penetrating stare. He nodded. "I appreciate that. But I meant what I said too. I don't want that to be how this ends. I suppose, I don't want to die a coward."

"Most people get as far as thinking *I don't want to die* and stop there."

McKendrick grinned. "Oh, don't get me wrong. I was a soldier when I was your age, and staying alive was high on my list of priorities too. Your perspective changes slightly as you get older. You accept that, like it or not, you're not going to be here forever, and all you can try to do is leave the place tidy and face whatever comes next with courage and optimism."

"You think something comes next?"

"How's your physics?" Horn looked at him like a joiner. "One of the cornerstones is the idea that mass and energy are different facets of the same thing, and you can alter it but you can't destroy it or make any more and the component parts are pretty much eternal. I imagine the component parts of me will be altered a fair bit by death, but the atoms at least will go on. It's a kind of afterlife. And maybe the atoms will remember." It was hard to tell from his expression if he was joking again.

Either way, it all sounded rather implausible to Horn. But then, as a way of holding things together, he thought you couldn't beat a dovetail. Even if he'd heard of it, the strong nuclear force would have left him unimpressed.

"And then," added McKendrick, "I'm not ready to buy what you're selling. You think we're all going to die. *I* think there's a lot of ways this could end. I spent a lot of money on the security here. If one man, however expert and determined, can breach it in a few hours, I'm going to have serious words with the company that installed it."

"Good luck with that," muttered Horn to McKendrick's descending back.

They'd reached the front hall. Beth had overheard the tail end of their conversation. "The company that installed the security here," she said pointedly, "advised you against squandering the goodwill of the local police by testing the speed of their response every few days."

"Well, that's true," admitted McKendrick. "Okay. We've got the Tablecloth of Truce flying over the battlements. And we've worked out a plan of campaign. Will you sit with William, Beth? Keep the phones with you—nip outside every few minutes and try for a signal. But be careful. It wouldn't take a genius to guess we'll be doing that. Keep low, behind the parapet.

"I'll man the screens, try to get some idea what he's doing. I'll have the baby monitor in here so if you need help upstairs, or if you see anything, or if you get a phone signal, you can let me know."

Beth nodded.

"And the other thing we can do," continued McKendrick, "is prepare some fallback positions. So if he gets inside the house, we can retreat and put some solid doors between us. Remember, that's what this house was designed to do. Long before there were steel shutters—long before there was steel—it was laid out in such a way that the defenders would always have the advantage over the attackers. Using your house as a weapon may be a bit of a lost art, but we'll get the hang of it. We have all the advantages—stone walls, steel shutters, CCTV, food and water. He has to make all the going. All we have to do is sit tight."

"For how long?"

"As long as it takes. Until something changes."

"You mean," said Beth flatly, "until he finds a way in and slits all our throats."

McKendrick regarded her coolly. "That would count, yes."

"And you're going to let it happen?" She was looking at Horn.

But McKendrick answered, and his tone left little room for argument. "No, Beth, he's going to do what you're going to do. You're both going to do what you're told. You're going to go sit with your uncle William, and Nicky's going to prepare some last-ditch defenses. Get together some things we can fight with if push comes to shove."

Horn thought that push would go a great deal further than shove but he'd already said so as clearly as he could. And maybe McKendrick was right. Maybe something would happen. Even hit men are only human: they get heart attacks, they get toothache, they get the trots. This was a good place to finish the job he'd been paid for, but if circumstances turned against him, he would know he could always find Horn again. He'd leave here before compromising his own safety or his client's identity. Maybe McKendrick was right, and all they had to do was make it really difficult for him.

Horn wished with all his heart that he could believe it. But he didn't. He thought he was going to die today and take with him some people who didn't deserve it. That was almost his biggest regret. He didn't want to die; but he didn't much want to go on living the way he had either. It left him with not much to lose. The McKendricks had more. If it was hardly worth the trouble of fighting for his own life anymore, something deep inside him told him it was worth fighting for them.

Courage and optimism, McKendrick had said. A man could have a worse epitaph. "Do you have any guns? Shotguns, sporting guns—anything?"

McKendrick shook his head. "Never saw much point in shooting at something that couldn't shoot back."

Horn had to laugh. It was that or go mad. "I wish everyone felt the same way. What about the simple stuff—swords, spears, bows and arrows?"

"Yeah, right," began McKendrick in tones of vast scorn; but the words dried in his mouth. A look of surprised appreciation stole into his eyes. "Yes. Of course. To me it's just medieval wallpaper, an apt way to decorate a castle, but that's not what it was designed for. It was designed to kill people. The Great Hall, on the first landing. Take anything you can find."

Horn took his toolbag with him. He assumed that, when you hung a morning star on the chimney breast, you relied on more than a picture hook and a bit of string to keep it there.

All things are comparative. In one of the grander castles, Warwick or Arundel for instance, Birkholmstead's Great Hall would have been little more than an anteroom. But it was the heart of McKendrick's little fortress. It occupied virtually the whole of the first floor, with long lancet windows on two sides and a fireplace where you could have roasted an ox if you could have got it up the stairs.

The views were nowhere near as spectacular as those from the tower, but then these windows weren't for looking out of. They were narrow enough to exclude attackers but wide enough for an archer; narrow enough that glazing them, even in medieval times, would not have been prohibitively expensive; and narrow enough that the strong stone walls between them had no difficulty carrying the floors above.

But even by the time Birkholmstead was built, no one of quality wanted to spend all day looking at a stone wall. They covered them with tapestries, with banners, with trophies—and with weapons.

Great long pikes that were the foot soldier's answer to a man on a galloping horse. The lance and saber that were the cavalryman's riposte. Corselets of chain mail, long ago turned to rusty knitting that would never again ripple like liquid armor however much WD-40 was applied. And bows. Elegant six-foot shafts of English yew, once the most devastating weapon in the world, and ugly composite crossbows that were heavy to carry and took perilously long to reload but could be mastered by any fighting man with rudimentary training. And maybe even by scribes and carpenters, if the need was pressing enough.

Much as he was drawn to the wood, Horn had to admit that none of these bows was ever going to fire again. The elegant longbows were warped and shriveled by the years, their strings long sundered, the ugly crossbows corroded to inaction. The quivers of cloth-yard shafts and punchy crossbow quarrels were fit only for decoration now, their points rusted together, their fletchings depredated by mites.

The swords, the lances, the pikes—and yes, there was a morning star—might still have something to offer. Not much of an edge anymore, perhaps, but five feet of Damascus steel swung with enough determination would still break bones and rend flesh. Even a man used to dispensing instant murder from a weapon the size of his hand might hesitate for just long enough when confronted by someone trying to take his head off with a broadsword.

With hacksaw and pliers, guiltily standing on furniture he knew to be priceless, Horn took them down from the walls and stacked them on the floor. Then he stood back, wondering how to deploy them.

And while he was looking, a strange thought stole over him.

In four years this was the first time, the very first time, that he'd considered fighting back. He'd hidden and he'd run, turn and turn about, until there was nowhere left to hide and nowhere to flee. But he still wouldn't have thought of fighting if he hadn't met Robert McKendrick. The ghost of a smile touched his lips. Every other challenge in his life he'd done battle with and, for the most part, defeated. Why had it taken a city slicker in an expensive suit to point out that he could fight this too? Maybe he couldn't win, but he had nothing left to lose by trying. He didn't have to accept his fate like a butcher's beast. He could go down fighting—if not like a cornered lion, at least like a seriously pissed-off ferret. It was a better way to die, and he owed that to McKendrick. It was a pity he was going to repay the gift by annihilating his family.

Except, of course, that he wasn't. He wasn't going to pull the trigger. He hadn't hired the man who was going to pull the trigger. Nothing he had done justified what Tommy Hanratty was going to do to him. He hadn't even done what Hanratty thought he'd done.

He straightened up and, leaving the cache of ancient weapons on the floor, walked quietly back downstairs.

McKendrick, flicking between cameras, barely looked up as Horn walked behind him. "Any luck?"

Horn didn't answer. "I need to tell you something."

Then McKendrick looked round. He hadn't imagined that odd note in the younger man's voice: there was an odd look in his eyes too. Not just the stress, that had been there all along, but something new. Something suspended halfway between urgency and resignation: a curiously intense calm. Not so much the calm of resolution, more what you find in the hearts of hurricanes. "All right."

"I know you don't really believe what I'm saying. That this is where it ends, and not just for me. I know you think that with a bit of effort and ingenuity there are other ways this could work out. And maybe you're right. I hope you are. But just for the moment, will you humor me? Will you consider the possibility that you're going to die today? You're going to die, and Beth's going to die, because you helped me when most people would just have kept walking."

Horn swallowed, but he wasn't finished. McKendrick waited.

"You didn't know who I was when you took the decision to get involved. You knew nothing about me. So maybe it doesn't too much matter to you that a lot of people wouldn't have thought my skin worth saving. Not just not worth risking your life for—not worth getting your hands dirty for. But it matters to me. I know you wish you'd never glanced up that alley. But since you did, and we can't change what's happened and we probably can't change what's going to happen, it also matters to me that you don't die thinking you threw it all away—all this, everything you've worked for—on trash.

"I want you to know the truth. I never meant to tell a soul. I meant to take it to my grave. But then, I never expected to be taking other people with me. I want you to know."

McKendrick genuinely had no idea what was coming. "Know what?"

"I didn't do it. I didn't cut Patrick's rope. Patrick cut it himself."

CHAPTER 8

To nicky horn it seemed as if he'd accidently hit McKendrick's off switch. The man froze where he sat, twisted round from the monitors, and the rigor went all the way from his eyes into the depths of his soul. For ten, maybe fifteen seconds—which is a lot longer than it sounds when you're waiting—he didn't move and he didn't speak. He didn't even blink.

Then he did. A moment later his voice returned as a hoarse croak. "Are you serious?"

Whatever Horn had expected—and he really hadn't known what kind of reaction his declaration would provoke—it wasn't that. His brows gathered in a troubled frown. "You think it's something I'd joke about?"

"Patrick Hanratty cut his own rope."

"Yes."

"You said he wasn't responding—that you thought he was dead. You thought he was dead, and when you couldn't hold him any longer you cut the rope."

"I lied."

"Damn sure you lied to somebody about something," snarled McKendrick. As his emotions defrosted, the one that thawed quickest was anger. "Why in God's name should I believe you this time?"

The only answer Horn had was the simple one. "Because it's the truth."

"That not only was Patrick not dead, he was still conscious and functioning. That's what you're telling me? But instead of trying to save himself, he cut the rope and fell to his death. *Why?*"

Horn's muscles were tense, his breath coming quicker. As if he were confessing something terrible, something that could bring down the sky. He wasn't. But he'd lived with the lies so long that he almost felt as if he was. "Because if he hadn't, he'd have pulled me off the mountain. I couldn't save him. But he could save me. He died alone so I didn't have to decide whether or not to die with him."

It wasn't so much disbelief that came flooding back into McKendrick's face as rank incredulity. He said it again, with added emphasis. "*Why?* If that's what happened, why did you tell people you cut him loose? Why would you tell a lie that made a coward of you? Why would you deny your friend his last act of courage?"

Horn gave an awkward little shrug. His voice was small. "I thought it was better. Kinder. I thought people—some people—his people—might call what he did suicide."

McKendrick's brow furrowed. He seemed to want to understand but was finding it uphill work. "It's not my idea of suicide. I wouldn't have thought it was anybody's, even an Irish Catholic's. Anyway, the Church takes a more compassionate view these days, and has done for twenty years. The Hanrattys could still have buried Patrick in the family plot even if on a strict interpretation his death could be considered suicide."

"They never got the chance to bury him," growled Horn. "He's still out on the mountain somewhere under Anarchy Ridge. Did you know his dad sent an expedition to recover the body? He thought it would prove what actually happened, as distinct from what I said happened. The funny thing is, he was right, it would—only, not the way he thought." But if it had been as funny as all that, you'd have expected at least one of them to be smiling.

McKendrick was still trying to get his head round it. "Hanratty thinks you *murdered* Patrick? That what happened wasn't an accident?"

"He thought it was murder however it happened. Patrick died and I lived, and that made it my fault. On top of that, he was convinced I was covering something up. That what I told the authorities wasn't what happened. And of course he was right—he was just wrong about what. He thought if he could recover the body he could prove it was more than just bad luck. I don't know what he expected to find. That I'd knifed him in the ribs? That I'd bound him hand and foot with my second-best rope and pushed him off Anarchy Ridge? I don't know. Anyway, by the time they climbed up there, too much snow had fallen and they couldn't find him. He's probably part of the glacier by now. But that's all right. Patrick would rather be buried in a glacier than a churchyard. So would I."

The silence went on and on—mountainous, glacial. Almost it became too big to break. Which was curious, because although these were matters of enormous import to Nicky Horn, McKendrick had no emotional investment in them. He was entitled to be surprised. But Horn was bewildered as to why a man who'd shown so little interest in what happened on Little Horse that he hadn't recognized Horn's face should be furious to learn now that what the dogs in the street knew to be true was, in fact, not. The anger, and the silence, said something else was going on in Robert McKendrick's head.

Eventually Horn gritted desperately, "Say something."

McKendrick sucked in a deep breath that broke the spell. He glared at Horn, eyes sparking with a rage that all the peril Horn had brought to his door had not aroused him to. "What? What would you like me to say? That's all right, then? That changes everything? I'm going to die—Beth's going to die—for a *lie*?"

Horn avoided looking at him. "So suddenly I'm right and we're all going to die?"

Instantly McKendrick was on his feet, looming, his height giving him a physical presence that Horn had hardly noticed when he was calm. He wasn't calm now. His fists were clenched and shaking. Had he—the other one, the man outside—suspected that this dangerous man dwelled inside the well-suited executive who interrupted him at his work, and was that why in the alley he'd backed down rather than call McKendrick's bluff? Because he knew—because it was his job to know—it wasn't actually a bluff?

"Why?" McKendrick demanded a third time. There was a rattle in his voice like the rattle of a railway track with a train coming. "Why would you tell people that, if it wasn't true?"

"I was trying to protect Patrick's family," mumbled Horn. "It was a hard thing to tell to them. They're not climbers, they wouldn't know that what he did made him a hero. They'd just know that, at a time when he still had an element of choice, he killed himself so that I could come home. I thought that would tear them apart. I thought it was better for them to resent a stranger than their own son."

"Resent you? They sent a hit man after you!" yelled McKendrick, all restraint gone. "You didn't think maybe *that* was the time to tell the truth?"

Horn shook his head stubbornly. "By then it was too late. We were way past the point where Tommy Hanratty was going to believe anything I said. Changing my story then wouldn't have done me any good, but it would have harmed Patrick."

"Patrick Hanratty died to save you having to! How was telling people *that* going to harm him?"

"Because . . ." Horn stopped abruptly. "You're right. Other climbers would have respected him for it. Maybe most rational people would. But not the people closest to him. They'd have thought that he'd put what I needed above what they needed—that he'd made a conscious decision to throw away any chance of coming back to them. That he'd chosen me above them. It would have colored all their memories of him forevermore. His mother, his sister, even his thug of a father—they'd never have been able to think of him without resenting that choice. Without wondering how necessary it was. Whether we really were out of options, or if he'd just had enough and couldn't take any more. Maybe that seems like a detail to you, but it wouldn't to the Hanrattys and it wouldn't to Patrick. Suicide wouldn't be just a word to any of them.

"You can laugh at people religious enough to think less of someone who died saving a friend, or you can get angry and throw things, but the fact is that if I said Patrick cut his own rope, that family would have choices to make between their son and their beliefs. There was time to think about it while I was hiking in, and I didn't see the need to put them through that. I owed Patrick better than the risk of being misunderstood." Horn looked up then, his eyes hot. "I didn't expect Hanratty to like me very much when he heard the story. But I sure as hell didn't expect him to kill me!"

"There was an inquest," remembered McKendrick. "Before you left Alaska. You lied to them?"

"I told the same story from the day I got back to civilization and reported Patrick's death. I'd worked out all the details in my head, gone over it so often it almost felt like the truth. I told the same thing to the Alaskan coroner and again to the police here when I got home." Horn dared a glance at McKendrick's face, but nothing he saw there reassured him. He struggled on. "I thought I was doing the right thing. Every time I served it up, it went down a little easier. A time came when I half believed it myself. I knew there'd be criticism. I knew some people would think what I'd done—what I said I'd done—was beyond the pale. But I thought that was the worst I'd have to deal with. I thought I could weather the storm. For Patrick? He'd died for me—I could lie for him."

"And now—*now!*—you feel this irresistible urge to set the record straight?"

"I owe you the truth. And I thought it was now or never."

Incredibly, McKendrick started to laugh. Almost hysterically, thought Horn; as if these events mattered more to him than they had any right to. He was at a loss to explain the intensity of the man's reaction.

"What?" Horn demanded at length. *"What?"*

"Sorry." McKendrick wiped a hand across his eyes, cleared his throat and forced a little decorum back into his manner. "It's just . . . this is so *not* how I expected to be spending today. Okay. You swear to me, this is the truth you're telling now?" Horn nodded. "Have you tried to tell Hanratty?"

Horn's eyebrows soared. "What's the point? He already thinks I'm a killer and a coward—it's not going to give him massive problems to think I'm a liar as well."

McKendrick let his head rock back, and in the second before he turned away Horn saw his eyes glaze over, as if everything was changed utterly by what he'd heard—that a climber's rope had been cut at one end rather than the other. "I need to think," he muttered, heading for the stairs. "Watch the monitors. If you see anything, yell."

"Believe it," mumbled Horn.

Beth was coming down the steps from the tower. They met outside William's room. "Trying the mobiles again?" asked McKendrick.

She nodded. "Still no joy. Which, of course, is why we have a landline—the mobiles have always been more miss than hit here."

"You'd think, from the roof . . ."

She held them out. "You want to try?"

McKendrick blew out his cheeks. "No. The only way to get any higher than the turret is to climb the flagpole, and while I'm sure I could do that if I really wanted, I doubt if I could do it one-handed while dialing with the other."

Beth gave a wan smile. "Supermack admits defeat?"

McKendrick smiled back but his manner was distracted. "Let's just say I'm looking for a plan with a higher success-to-effort ratio."

They went into William's room. McKendrick gave his brother

a friendly grin out of habit. The frozen man held him in an unwinking stare.

Beth had been sitting on the sofa. She put the phones down on the coffee table. McKendrick took the window seat. "What do you make of Nicky Horn?"

Beth's eyes flew wide with indignation. "You're asking *me*? You know what I think of him. You know why."

"I'm not sure I do."

She stared at him, hurt and uncomprehending. "Patrick was my friend. You know what it meant to lose him."

"Patrick died where he did, how he did, because that's where he chose to be. No one forced him to go to Alaska—I don't think even Tommy Hanratty thinks Horn drove him up Anarchy Ridge at gunpoint. Which makes his death sad and regrettable, but I'm not sure it makes it a tragedy. And I don't think it makes it Horn's responsibility."

"He cut Patrick's rope! How much more responsible can you get?!"

"Suppose," said McKendrick slowly, "just for a minute suppose, it all happened exactly as Horn told the inquiry. That Patrick fell, and he tried to pull him up, and he couldn't. And Patrick wasn't able to help. He might already have been dead, killed by the fall; or if he was still alive, he was hanging in space with an Alaskan blizzard howling round him. The warmest kit in the world wasn't going to protect him from that forever. Isn't the reality that, with just the two of them on the mountain, Patrick was dead the moment he slipped off the ridge?"

"Maybe he was," Beth retorted furiously. "But he didn't have to die alone."

McKendrick's head tilted as he tried to see into her soul. "Is that what you really believe? That it would have been better for both of them to die? That when Horn had done everything in his power to save his friend, and it wasn't enough, he was honor-bound to stay there until he too froze to death?"

"Yes!"

"Would you have felt the same way if it was Patrick who came back?"

That seemed to jolt her. As if it was a question she'd never asked herself. Her lips moved, but for a moment no words came. When she found a voice, it was low. "That's not fair. Patrick was my friend. Honestly? I wouldn't have cared who died on the mountain if Patrick had come back."

Her father was watching her with a degree of compassion that made her feel like a child again. She knew he was a tough man, she knew he was a clever man. She'd all but forgotten how much he loved her. "Beth—Patrick was more than just a friend, wasn't he?"

She didn't answer. But by then she didn't have to. Her eyes had filled up in a way that, four years on, could only be explained one way.

McKendrick said softly, "Why didn't you tell me?"

"Because . . ." She hesitated on the brink, unable to say the killer words.

"What?"

"Because I loved him forever. Because I never loved anyone else like that, and never wanted to. Because nothing in the world mattered to me as much as Patrick—the sound of his footstep, the touch of his hand, the kindnesses, the silly grin, the way laughter danced in his eyes . . . I didn't know you could love someone that much."

Her father reached out a long-fingered hand and laid it over hers, a gentle comforting weight. Only four years too late. "I'm so sorry."

"I should have told you."

"I shouldn't have needed telling. Then, or since."

"You understand, then? Why . . ."

"Of course I do. Quite apart from anything Horn did or didn't do on Anarchy Ridge, you blamed him for taking Patrick away from you. For taking him somewhere you couldn't go, and coming back without him. The point is not that Patrick was doing what he wanted to do. The point is, he wasn't doing what you wanted him to do."

"No." There was a note of relief in her sigh. Finally, a little understanding . . .

"If he'd come back—"

She interrupted swiftly, smothering the question at birth. "Who knows? People's feelings change. It might just have been one of those college things that burned out when we moved on and our horizons widened."

"But you don't think so."

Her gaze was lowered, her tone at once soft and unyielding. "I know what I felt."

McKendrick rolled his eyes to the ceiling. "I should never have brought him here. Horn. It was stupid—thoughtless. I should at least have kept you out of it."

Now she looked at him curiously. "You could have stayed out of it yourself."

"I thought I was doing the right thing. I didn't anticipate any of this. Not that someone would come here. And not what you've just told me. I wish to God I'd done things differently."

Beth gave an odd, affectionate little chuckle. "It's so unlike you, somehow. Acting on impulse. You're always so . . . calculating. Sorry. Does that sound rude?"

"Not rude. Not exactly flattering either," said McKendrick ruefully.

"It's true though. Usually you have all the details of the deal lined up before you pick up the phone. You know what you'll say, and what the other party'll say, and what your response will be. And you have contingencies ready in case he says something else. It's a pity, really, that when you finally do the human thing and reach out on the spur of the moment to help someone in trouble, it's someone who isn't worth saving and it's liable to get us all killed."

He'd known her all her life, and half of his. Today he was learning things about her that stunned him to the marrow of his bones. One was the harshness of her view of him.

But maybe she was right. Their predicament was entirely of his making, and he hadn't even the excuse she credited him with—a spontaneous act of philanthropy. It had happened because he was doing what he always did, what his daughter knew he always did—playing both sides of the chessboard.

He couldn't tell her that. He diverted the conversation down the other avenue. "You think Horn's right, then? We're not going to walk away from this?"

For a moment she hesitated; then she shook her head. "No, I don't. The only one who's in any danger here is him. He wants us to think otherwise because he hopes we'll be scared enough to protect him." She managed a wan smile. "How about you? Are you updating your will?"

Though he didn't share her analysis, he did share her conclusion.

"No. For one thing there's no need—it all comes to you. But don't hold your breath. I'm not ready to part with it just yet."

Beth's smile turned impish. "You reckon we can keep him out, then—Tommy Hanratty's hit man?"

"I think so. Long enough for him to think the balance of risk and reward is shifting. He isn't Henry the Fifth at Harfleur—he isn't going to lose a kingdom if he can't breach the walls. Horn is a job to him, that's all. If he can't do it today, he'll do it next week. He won't risk his own safety literally banging his head against a stone wall."

"Horn thinks he will."

"Nicky Horn is an exhausted, frightened young man who's been on the run for four years. His judgment shouldn't be relied on."

"He isn't exaggerating about Tommy Hanratty," Beth said quietly. "He's a seriously vicious man. Patrick was terrified of him. If he wants Horn dead, sooner or later, one way or another, it's going to happen. You can't save him. All you can do is try to keep him from dying here, and it's not worth antagonizing someone like Hanratty to do that. Possibly not for anyone; certainly not for Horn."

McKendrick drew a deep breath. He was going to have to tell her. She had persuaded herself that, even if it wasn't lawful, even if the morality of it was suspect, there was a kind of justice in Nicky Horn's dying at the will of Patrick Hanratty's father. She needed to know that her feelings about Horn were predicated on a lie. Somewhat to his dismay, McKendrick found he couldn't guess how she would react. If she would believe Horn's latest account. If believing would add to her grief or ease it. A man should know his daughter well enough to know if he was bringing her balm or brimstone. It troubled him that they had so many secrets from one another.

He'd only ever wanted what was best for her. He was afraid now that he didn't know her well enough to judge.

He said, "Will you answer me one question honestly?" She nodded. "What if Patrick had cut Nicky Horn's rope?"

Beth frowned. "I told you that already. If only Patrick had come home, I'd have felt sorry for Patrick."

McKendrick knuckled his eyes. "Then surely to God you can understand—"

She didn't let him finish. "You asked for an honest answer and that was it. Patrick was the only one I cared about—Patrick, right or wrong. If he'd pushed Horn off the mountain because he wanted his climbing boots, I'd still have sided with Patrick. Nicky Horn could go to hell in a handcart and I wouldn't have broken a nail to save him—and that's not just now, that's always. It's no use asking me for an unbiased opinion, I'm not capable of giving one. I loved one of them. I didn't give a damn about the other, until he ruined my life.

"But if you're asking whether it's ever all right for one climber to cut another's rope, the answer's no, and that doesn't alter regardless of who lives and who dies. We all carry a knife. We all know that if the game turns nasty enough, if it comes to a choice between one person dying and two people dying, we may have to cut ourselves loose so that someone else can live. But that's it—you only ever cut your own rope. Whatever the consequences, you never cut someone else's. You haven't the right."

"Is that—I don't know—an unwritten rule? Something all climbers agree on?"

"Maybe not all. But it's the sort of thing you discuss in the bar at the end of a long hard climb, and everyone I ever climbed with, everyone whose opinion I respected, felt that they'd rather die than kill someone else."

"Maybe," McKendrick suggested softly, "it's a conclusion that's easier to come to in the bar at the end of a climb than halfway up a mountain in a howling gale."

"No doubt. That's why you talk about these things first. You take your decisions when you're safe and warm and calm, so you don't have to take them when you're frantic and freezing and scrambling on the edge of an abyss. All you have to do then is remember and act on them."

"And cut your own rope if you have to."

"If you have to," she agreed grimly. "If there's no way back that doesn't involve ending someone else's life. It's a risk sport, Mack. If you're not prepared to take the risks, you shouldn't be on the mountain. You shouldn't be on someone's rope if you're prepared to kill them with it."

"So cutting your own rope wouldn't count as suicide?"

She snorted a derisive laugh. "Of course not. Among climbers it's the ultimate act of courage."

"I wonder if climbers' families see it that way."

She became aware that the conversation had changed, was no longer about what she thought and felt, wasn't sure what it was about now. She looked at him sideways, one eyebrow higher than the other. "Mack?"

It was one of those now-or-never moments. McKendrick steeled himself. "Horn says Patrick cut his own rope. When he couldn't climb back, and Horn couldn't lift him, and it was a choice of one or both of them staying on the mountain, Patrick found the courage to cut his own rope. Horn edited the facts to spare his family's feelings."

Beth's expression had frozen on her face. McKendrick hurried on. "Of course, he'd no idea the trouble he was getting himself into. He thought that, from their point of view, the easiest thing to deal with was if Patrick died in the fall and Horn had to leave his body behind. So that's what he said.

"He thought he was doing the right thing, Beth. He came up with a story that allowed Patrick's family to grieve without reservation, in the hope that the people whose opinion mattered most to him would understand. He was questioned in Alaska; he was questioned again when he got back to England. He stuck to the account he'd worked out. There was no way of proving anything different, no reason to suspect he was lying. No witnesses, no forensics—as long as he didn't blink, the authorities had to accept what he told them."

Still no response from his daughter. Not from her lips and not from her eyes. McKendrick sighed. "What he didn't allow for was the fact that Patrick's family was headed not just by a grieving father but by a grieving thug of a father. *He* didn't have to accept what he was told simply because there was no evidence to the contrary. And he didn't have to nurse his doubts in the darkness of his own soul, powerless to do anything about them. He did what he was in a habit of doing whenever somebody crossed him. He set about making Horn pay."

It was amazing to McKendrick—alarming, even—that he'd been able to get the story out without interruption. He'd expected to have to fend off furious interjections and battle to the end through his daughter's distress and disbelief. Her silent stare unnerved him. But he didn't want to prompt her. He wanted to give her all the time she needed to absorb what he'd said and make sense of how she felt about it.

Finally she favored him with a cool smile and said calmly, "Well, he saw you coming, didn't he?" As if he'd been sold a race-horse with four left feet.

"I think it's the truth," he managed, suddenly defensive.

She shook her head bemusedly. "For a hardheaded business-man, you're a mug for a sob story. Of course it isn't the truth. We know what the truth is. It's what he told the authorities in Alaska and again when he got back here. Do you think they wouldn't have realized if he was lying to them? All their experience dealing with thieves and murderers, and they're going to have the wool pulled over their eyes by a carpenter with a warped sense of right and wrong? Grow up, Mack. He said he cut Patrick loose because that's what happened. He thought nobody could touch him for it. He's come up with this other version because his back's against the wall and he thinks you can help him, but only if he can convince you he's worth helping. Well, maybe he has convinced you. He'll have to try a lot harder to convince me."

He'd expected her to resist the idea. He'd expected tears and tantrums. Her calm dismissal of Horn's new account made him wonder if he'd accepted it too readily. "It seemed to make sense," he mumbled lamely.

"What?" Her arrow-straight gaze almost knocked him off his seat. "That because the Hanrattys are Catholics they couldn't be ex-pected to see the difference between their son committing suicide as an act of despair and giving up his life to save his friend? How stupid do you think they are? No, don't answer that—about as stupid as

Horn thinks you are! Why do you think he waited until you were alone before he told you that? Because he knew I'd see it for what it is. I don't claim to be a theologian, but doesn't all that stained-glass commemorate martyrs of one kind or another? People who gave their lives to help other people? If the Catholic Church regarded them all as suicides, I don't think they'd be up there in their windows."

McKendrick had to admit that she was right. Even he, with less knowledge of religious dogma than he had of the dark side of the moon, could see all the difference in the world between despair and self-sacrifice. When you tried to analyze it, it made no sense. If Horn had misled the police about what happened, sparing the Hanrattys' feelings wasn't why. "You think he's lying?"

She laughed out loud, a jarring discordance. "Of course he's lying, Mack! It's what he does, remember? Even on his own account, he's lied to someone. Look. He had no reason to tell the police what he did if it wasn't true. At best he was going to make himself unpopular, at worst it was going to get him into trouble. Whereas lying to you now just might buy him a bit more time. So which do you reckon is most likely? Patrick cut the rope and Horn said he did it? Or Horn cut the rope and toughed it out until it looked as though a different story would serve him better? We know what he does when he's staring death in the face. Anything he can think of to keep himself safe a little bit longer. Do you really think that a man who left his best friend on Anarchy Ridge would draw the line at lying to someone he met a few hours ago?"

"I suppose not," McKendrick muttered. A pit was in the middle of him where his heart had sunk. You couldn't blame a man for doing anything he had to in the effort to survive. Still somehow he was terribly disappointed.

It took him another minute to realize that, actually, this was a good thing. A Nicky Horn who'd lied to protect his friend's reputation wouldn't be much use to him. What he needed for his purposes was the young man Beth and the world thought he was—someone who prized his own survival so highly he'd do whatever it demanded of him. Anarchy Horn. That lingering sense of disappointment was sheer sentimentality, and McKendrick had never been a sentimental man. His long jaw hardened. "Stupid of me," he gritted. "You're right, of course."

"Of course," she echoed softly. "So you'll do as I ask? Stop protecting him?"

McKendrick's eyes turned inward for a moment, searching his conscience, examining his hopes and plans. Beth hardly noticed that what he said was not an echo of what she'd said. "I have no desire to protect him," he growled.

CHAPTER 9

MCKENDRICK WAS ANGRY and didn't want to see Horn for a while. Beth suggested that they swap shifts—that she go downstairs and watch the monitors and he sit quietly with his brother for a space. She went up the tower with the mobile phones first, came back shaking her head. "Still no joy."

"They never used to be this bad."

"Name me something that did."

There was no arguing with that. McKendrick nodded. "Give me fifteen minutes to get my head sorted, then I'll come down."

"Shall I tell him to go?"

"No," said McKendrick grimly. "Leave it to me."

"As you prefer." She closed William's door softly behind her.

Horn was watching the monitors in the stone hall. He spoke before looking round, before he knew it was her. "I caught a movement on the far side of the courtyard five minutes ago. Nothing since."

"Maybe he's given up and gone home."

Horn turned quickly at Beth's voice, and as quickly turned back. "Somehow I doubt it," he said gruffly to the screens.

"Maybe you should go outside and check. We'd feel pretty silly starving to death in here if he'd gone away days before."

"Tell you what. Before we starve to death, I will."

"Fine," said Beth airily. "Or now. Whichever."

Over the screens Horn's back was hunched and tense, as if he anticipated an assault. "That's really what you want, is it? To see me die. Will that satisfy you? Is it the only thing that will? Do you need to see me die before you can get on with your life?"

She considered for a moment. "No, not really. I'd settle for hearing it from a reliable source."

He gritted his teeth. "And you think that's what Patrick would want?"

"When he was alive? Of course not. He liked you, he trusted you—he wouldn't have climbed with you if he hadn't. But you cut him loose. In the four or five seconds it took him to meet up with the mountain again, I think he may have revised his opinion."

Finally Horn made himself look at her. "Mack didn't tell you?"

"Your latest attempt at self-justification?" Her tone was scornful. "That, in contrast to everything you've told everyone for the last four years, in fact Patrick cut his own rope? Yes, he told me. I think, for a few innocent minutes, he actually believed it. Then reality intervened. What amazed me was that it took a few minutes. He's not considered gullible in the City."

"I'm not trying to justify myself," growled Horn mulishly. "It's the truth."

"Of course it is. Along with fairy godmothers, the Loch Ness Monster, the yeti, and the alien autopsies. After all, what possible reason could you have to lie?"

Horn swiveled his chair to meet her gaze full on. "And why do you find it so hard to believe that a man you call your friend, someone you say you were close to, did what we all hope we'd be brave enough to do in the same circumstances? Patrick Hanratty died well. Why are you so determined to take that from him?"

"Why were you?" she countered swiftly. "If it was such a good death, why did you tell people that you dropped him off the mountain like a pack that got too heavy to carry?"

He looked away. It may have been disdain, but it looked as if he couldn't bear her scrutiny. "His family . . ."

"His family are Catholics," retorted Beth, "not stupid. If it had happened the way you say—the way you say *now*—they'd have been proud of him. Even the old thug. You *knew* who he was—what he does, how he does it. And you announced that you'd cut his son's rope. You must have known how he'd react to that. You must at least have wondered if he'd come after you with a flamethrower. But that was the story you told, and that was the story you stuck to. If you'd been lying, you could have come up with something so much better. The only possible reason for telling Tommy Hanratty that you cut Patrick's rope was that it was the truth."

"No."

"Nobody lies to get themselves into *more* trouble! It's perfectly obvious what happened. You told the Alaskans what happened exactly as it happened because you were so relieved to be alive that you couldn't see anything wrong with it. I don't think it occurred to you that you'd be pilloried for what you'd done. You thought the old macho climbing establishment would see it your way: that when it's a matter of survival, you're entitled to do anything you have to. Even killing a friend."

"Well, it may have kept you on the right side of the law, just, but the law isn't the only arbiter of a man's actions. The first, the really important one, is his own conscience. And if that isn't up to the job, there's a kind of human morality that most people share, that tells them how they should behave even in circumstances beyond their worst nightmares. That tells them *this* and *this* are all right if there's really no alternative, but *this* isn't to be contemplated even if it means the sky must fall. What you did was way beyond anything decent human beings consider acceptable."

She paused, watching Horn's face. She saw the strong muscles of his jaw clench and the dull flush that assured her that her carefully aimed darts were finding their target. That four years hadn't been enough to blunt their barbs. "You and Patrick went to Anarchy Ridge together. He fell, and you held him. I'm sure you did try to pull him up; but he was a big guy, bigger than you, and if he was a dead weight—if he was unconscious, or hurt, and he couldn't help—I can see how you wouldn't be able to do it. Which was a shitty position to find yourself in. You must have gone over it again and again in your mind, holding him while your muscles cracked with the effort, trying to find a third way."

It was as if she'd been there. As if she'd witnessed what happened. More than that: as if she'd been inside his head, seeing through his eyes, feeling what he felt, running desperately through all the options and brought up short by the realization that none of them would serve.

"You could have lowered him," she said. "But that ridge drops away sheer into nothing, doesn't it? I've seen the pictures. No one carries enough rope for a contingency like that. You could have made the rope fast to a tree or a rock. But there aren't any trees up there, and the rocks were under a meter of ice. You could yell for help and hope someone heard you. But that's kind of the point of wild climbing, isn't it? Going places where there aren't guidebooks, and there aren't belays hammered into the rocks. Having nothing and no one to depend on but yourselves. And it was wild climbing that attracted you. You and Patrick, you *liked* going where no one could help you. However much you yelled, no one was going to hear you.

"Finally you were back to the same two choices you started with. Guess what? You picked the wrong one."

"I couldn't save him," muttered Horn insistently. "I tried. I couldn't pull him up."

"I believe you. I think you did try to haul him up, and found you couldn't. Maybe no one could have done." But it wasn't absolution in her voice. There was something implacable about her calm. She was no longer watching him through eyes red-rimmed with hatred. She was looking at him like looking down a microscope. Studying, analyzing, noting his deficiencies. "But you had to decide what to do next. If he'd been dead, it would have been easy enough. But Anarchy Ridge wasn't going to be that kind to you. Patrick had fallen, but there was nothing around him but snow and wind— nothing to kill himself on. You could hear him shouting over the storm, couldn't you? Telling you he was okay, give or take the odd cracked rib, waiting for you to help him. Demanding to know what was taking so long when he was freezing his nuts off. There was never a moment when you thought he was dead on your rope, or even badly injured. Was there?"

Beth raised an interrogative eyebrow at him. When Horn didn't reply she shrugged and continued. "As time passed he must have realized you couldn't do it. That it was just asking too much. Maybe if you'd had more equipment. But you liked climbing fast and loose, without all the fancy paraphernalia that would let you take your granny up Everest. It's a wonder you were on a rope at all. A wonder and, as far as you were concerned, a disaster. But you were: he was at one end of it and you were at the other. And sooner or later you were going to weaken and lose your grip, and you'd fall off the mountain together."

Her strong jaw rose till she was literally looking down her nose at him. "Did you ask him to cut the rope? Did you ask him to take his knife out and cut himself free? Did you put it to him sensibly, rationally, pointing out that you'd done your best but there was no way off the mountain for both of you? And when he couldn't bring himself to do it, did you get angry and shout at him? *Cut the rope. You know what you have to do. Cut the fucking rope! Cut the rope, or I will—*"

"For God's sake!" The words came from Nicky Horn as if wrung out by torture. "You don't know. You *can't* know—how it was, what it was like. He fell. I tried to pull him up but I couldn't. That high, and that cold, you haven't the same strength. It was all I could do to hold on to him. For three hours we just stayed there, him hanging in midair, me hanging on to the mountain. I carved steps in the snow, to brace my feet against, but they kept giving way under the weight. After half an hour I knew I was weakening—I wasn't suddenly going to start getting stronger. Something that was beyond me at the start wasn't going to become possible as I got colder and more exhausted. Half an hour in we both knew how it was going to end. That there was no chance of help coming however long we waited. But the decision was his to take. After three hours he took it."

Beth tossed her chestnut braid like an impatient horse. "Do you know something, Horn? I'd almost be tempted to believe you. Patrick was a brave man. He was a kind, brave man and I could believe he'd cut his own rope rather than see you die trying to save him after all hope was gone. I'd have no trouble believing that, except for one thing. You. You're not even a good liar. Every word you say, every lie you tell, makes it perfectly clear what happened up there.

"It *was* Patrick's decision. But you couldn't wait for him to make it, could you? You thought you could die waiting. You already had your knife out, to carve steps in the snow. And there was the rope right in front of you. It didn't even need a conscious action, just a slip of the hand. And then he was falling."

When she looked in Horn's eyes, it was almost possible to believe she could see what had happened mirrored there—the big man dangling helplessly on the taut rope, the smaller one fighting to hold it, the wink of sunshine on steel. Then Horn blinked and tears were on his face.

Beth McKendrick didn't care about his pain. After four years she was still too wrapped up in her own. She drove on relentlessly. "Maybe, for a split second, he misunderstood. He thought he'd pulled you off the mountain, and as he fell he'd see you come crashing over the cornice. But all he saw was the end of the rope. And in that moment he knew what you'd done. The last seconds of his life were filled with the knowledge that his best friend had killed him.

"Did he curse you as he fell? Did he damn you to hell? I would have done," she assured him earnestly. "But this was Patrick. Maybe he used his last breath to forgive you. Is that the terrible secret you've been carrying round for four years? That with his last breath

Patrick forgave you for killing him? Is that why you had to lie and say he was dead on the rope when anyone who's seen a picture of Anarchy Ridge would know he couldn't have been? And why you had to stick with the lie even if it meant Tommy Hanratty putting a price on your head? Because if Patrick was alive and conscious, people would ask what you said to one another."

"No," whispered Nicky Horn.

"Then what? You've admitted he was conscious. You say he knew what he was doing and did what he had to. He must have said something. What were his last words?"

"Nothing," mumbled Horn.

"Oh, come on! He knew he was going to die. If this is finally the truth, he knew he was going to die a hero. He'd three hours to work out what he wanted to say, what he wanted people to remember him by. To make any explanations he felt necessary. So what did he say? After he fell, and before he fell to his death. What did he say to you?"

"I don't remember."

"*Of course you bloody remember!* The words must be seared into your brain like the brand on a beef steer's bum. Tell me what he said."

Once again she'd pushed him to the point where something inside Horn changed. Where he stopped backing away from his problems and turned on them with bared teeth. Where his manner went from secretive and defensive to belligerent, almost in the blink of an eye. He spun the chair in front of the monitors, rounding on her, and his voice was terse and barred with anger.

"You want to know what he said? His famous last words? You're sure? Then I'll tell you. Don't expect to like them. I don't think Patrick Hanratty was entirely the man you took him for.

"He worried about that. He knew he was going to end up disappointing you—hurting you. Oh yes, we talked about you. There's a lot of hours on a climb when you're not actually climbing, when it's dark outside or there's a blizzard keeping you inside the tent, and you huddle together for a bit of warmth and you talk. About mountains and girls." He cast her a tight, savage little grin. "Mostly about mountains. But when you've relived every ascent you've ever made, together and separately, finally the conversation turns to sex. Who you've had. Who you've wanted but couldn't have. Who wanted you.

"And yes, your name came up. He cared for you, he really did, but not how you cared for him. That's what bothered him. He knew that, however lightly he tried to let you down, you were going to feel betrayed. He wanted to keep your friendship, but he didn't think he was going to be able to. Things had gone too far. Friendship was never going to be enough for you. Patrick agonized over how he was going to tell you that the way you felt about him, he felt about someone else."

Beth recoiled as if he'd hit her. Her cheek was white. She'd known, of course—somewhere in her heart she'd known. She hadn't wanted to admit it to herself, and after Patrick died she never had to. She certainly hadn't expected it to be used against her by someone with whom she was locked in a kind of mortal combat. All she could find to say was what she'd been saying all along—"I don't believe you!"—and all she could find to say it with was a breathless ghost of a voice.

"Yes, you do," retorted Horn fiercely. "You know you and Patrick were never going to settle down and raise two-point-four children and a cocker spaniel. You knew it long before we went to Alaska. You just didn't want to face it. His death saved you from having to. And—be honest—there was just a little bit of relief mixed in with the sadness, wasn't there? Because now you could live the fantasy and there was no one, there was never going to *be* anyone, to call you a liar."

She slapped his face, as hard as she could. But though he rocked, his eyes barely left hers. They burned with a kind of bitter victory. Beth would have given her right arm to believe that this too was a lie, but she knew better. Mainly because he was right—none of it came as a surprise to her. She'd locked it away where she'd never expected to revisit it, but she'd known before Patrick died that they were in trouble. That he was being kind when he should have been honest. She'd known he wasn't happy. Like a coward, she'd hoped he'd never summon up the courage to tell her. That it was over between them; or rather, it had never been what she wanted, but she'd blinded herself to the facts because she wanted it so much.

If Patrick had lived, sooner or later they'd have had to confront it. That would have been the end, not only of the future Beth had wanted for them but also of the one Patrick hoped for. She'd loved him too much to remain friends, to meet up for the occasional drink after work and send christening cards to one another's children. If he'd lived, she'd have lost him. His death had spared her that.

"Except that there was. Me. I knew everything about you and Patrick," said Horn, "because he told me. Those cold windy nights in the mountains, after we'd talked about the really important stuff like overhangs and traverses, he told me what was going on in his life. I really wasn't that interested. I nodded and agreed with him from time to time, but mostly I was planning the next day's climb or sorting out my ropes or whatever. I liked the guy, I had a lot of time for him as a climber and he was good company in a bivouac, but I can't honestly say I was riveted by his love life. I listened with half an ear, to be polite."

He managed a little smile. "Looking back, I think maybe I was a bit dim. I'm not good at social chitchat, mainly because if it doesn't involve ropes and pitons I can't work up much interest. But I should have paid more attention. Maybe then I'd have put it together. Maybe what he said that last night in the tent wouldn't have come as such a goddamned shock."

His eyes still hadn't shifted from her face, and Beth felt somehow helpless to break their hold. She didn't know what was coming. She was pretty sure she wasn't going to like it. There seemed no possible way now to avoid it.

"You want me to tell you his famous last words? What he said as he cut the rope? You're sure—you really want to know? We can keep the genie in the bottle: we can't put it back once it's out. Do you want me to tell you what Patrick said before he fell?"

She whispered, "Yes."

Between the bruises Horn's weather-darkened face was the gray of old leather, but his eyes blazed like a hawk's. There was no longer any kind of victory there, though, only grief and excoriating remembrance. The words came thick in his throat. "He said he loved me."

CHAPTER 10

"YOU'RE LYING."

Beth couldn't imagine who'd spoken. It didn't sound like her voice; and in fact it wasn't saying what she believed. She'd have given anything to think that this was the lie and one of the other stories he'd told—*any* of them—was the truth. But it explained things for which she'd never had an explanation before. She'd known things weren't right between them. At the same time she'd known Patrick cared for her, wouldn't want to hurt her. She'd known, somewhere in her heart, that there was someone else. But she'd told herself that Patrick Hanratty wasn't the kind of man to play away—that if he was in love with someone else, or just didn't like her enough anymore, he'd have been honest with her. He wouldn't have let her go on thinking there was a future for them.

But what if it wasn't another girl he'd fallen in love with? Maybe he hadn't known how to tell her, or even what to tell her. Maybe he hadn't known himself whether this was a passing madness or the way his life was turning. Maybe he didn't want to say anything about it, not even to her, until he understood better himself what was going on. Didn't want to lose her, and shock and alienate his family—including his thug of a father—until he could still the turmoil in his brain enough to work out what he wanted and what he could reasonably expect to have.

He'd never expected to die on Anarchy Ridge, leaving her with so much unfinished business she'd been unable to move on with her life.

Horn grinned savagely. "Of course I'm lying. The trick is knowing which are the lies and which is the truth."

"This is a lie." It *was* Beth's voice, but she knew as she said it that she was lying too.

"If that's what you want to believe."

"Patrick loved me . . ."

"I know he did. But it wasn't your name he was yelling as he fell into the blizzard."

"You bastard." The whole of her body was shaking cold, except for the hot tears that spilled onto her cheeks. "You took him from me. *You?*"

Horn forced a dismissive laugh. "*I* didn't want him. Except on my rope; except for a friend. I'd never thought of Patrick that way. I didn't know he was thinking of me that way. When he talked about you and someone else, I thought he meant another girl. I'd have paid a bit more attention if I'd thought he meant me!"

"You didn't even *want* him? I *loved* him!"

Horn shrugged. He may have hoped to convey nonchalance, lack of concern, even a little man-of-the-world amusement. But he wasn't a man of the world—not in that sense, anyway. He was a joiner and a climber. He was a practical man, no good at nuances, bothered by complications. His casual shrug came across as awkward, gauche and uncouth. "But it wasn't about either of us, was it? Either you or me. It was about Patrick and what he wanted. How he saw his life shaping up.

"I damn near fell off the mountain when he told me. This was earlier, in the tent. The night before." Horn didn't have to specify what datum he was using. "I told him he was backing the wrong horse—that he was a great climber and a terrific all-round guy, but he wasn't my idea of a good lay." He swallowed. "In fact, I said rather more than that. Things I shouldn't have said—things I wouldn't have said if I'd had a bit more warning. Hurtful things.

"He apologized, said he understood—he was just telling me how he felt, he wasn't expecting anything from me in return. I think he was pretty shocked himself that he'd come out and said it. I don't know how long he'd been working up to it—if he'd always meant to come clean while we were in Alaska, or if it got away from him in an unguarded moment. I'd no idea it was anywhere in his mind until he said the words.

"And after he did, we never really got the chance to talk about it. He'd said all he wanted to, and so had I—too much. We avoided looking at one another for the rest of the night. Maybe if the next day had ended differently, we'd have got round to talking. We'd have had to if we wanted to keep climbing together. Or maybe we'd have got home and gone our separate ways—I don't know. We're never going to know, now."

Tell a woman that the man she was in love with loved another man and you do more than just set the record straight. You turn her view of the world, and her own place within it, on end.

Being left for another woman is upsetting, offensive, demeaning—however kind the man is, however gently he tries to let her down, the cold, hard, inescapable fact is that, whatever at-tracted him to her in the first place, she doesn't have enough of it and he's met someone who has more. It's worse than being the kid who's never picked for team games. It's like being picked, tried out, and then sent back to mind the pullovers.

Now imagine being the kid who's given a tryout, then told he played so badly that not only is he not getting a place on the team but the team's out of the league and the owner of the ball is going to go play with it in another park.

Every emotion in the lexicon flickered across Beth McKend-rick's face, but none of them settled for more than a moment. There was of course shock. There was outrage, and disbelief. There was ridi-cule. Then incredulity lifted a corner of its petticoats to give a glimpse of the mental turmoil beneath, as if she was at least trying to ac-knowledge the possibility. But it was too hard a truth to face, and she slammed back into the comfort of her default position, which was anger. It stiffened her sinews and suffused her cheeks with blood, but it didn't reach all the way up to her eyes. Her eyes were appalled, and terribly wounded, and they believed.

Beth McKendrick and Nicky Horn stared at one another across the unbearable truth—the young woman who'd have been willing to die for Patrick Hanratty's love and the young man who wasn't, both their lives blighted by a biological quirk that should barely have been worth comment except that a lack of honesty about it had woven filaments of kindness and misunderstanding, and the desperate attempt to avoid causing pain had trapped them all as surely as a gill net traps fish.

"He told you that?" Beth was struggling for the words. "That I loved him, and he loved you?"

"Yes."

She went on staring at him, humiliation rising to join the maelstrom in her eyes. "What did you do? Laugh?"

"No." He wasn't laughing now either. "There was nothing to laugh about. What he said—the way he was feeling—it knocked me sideways. Multiply what you're feeling now by about three and you're still not close. I thought I knew him, and it turned out I hardly knew him at all. And the thing about being in a tent in a snowstorm halfway up a mountain is, you can't stalk out and slam the door and be on your own until you've got your head together. We were going to be sleeping within reach of one another. Other times on other mountains we'd shared a sleeping bag to stay warm. You can imagine how *that* was going through my mind."

"You mean, you really didn't know? Until that trip—that night under Anarchy Ridge?"

Horn nodded grimly. "I had no idea. Maybe there were clues, but I was never any good at picking up what people aren't actually telling me. I thought we were talking about him and you. I'd no idea we were talking about him and you, and me."

"And when you did?"

He looked away. His voice was almost inaudible. "I called him a freak."

Most everyone who ever met him liked Patrick Hanratty. There was a gentleness about him, a sensitivity, a native inborn kindness, that made it hard not to. Everyone who knew about his background marveled that his father had managed first to sire such a son, then to raise him without trampling all that tenderness underfoot. The truth was, of course, that Patrick carried the imprint of his father's boots on his soul every day of his short life. He was afraid of his father every day. University had been the best time of his life because it was the longest time he was beyond the old thug's reach. He took to climbing for the same reason. Halfway up a mountain he had only the wind and the ice and the possibility of avalanches to worry about.

If he'd lived long enough he'd have got away, got far away with a woman, or a man, that he cared about, and the towering terror of his childhood would have faded to a mere distant shadow. But he was only twenty-three when he died. There hadn't been time for him to fulfill any of his potentials. The abiding love of old friends was the only memorial he left.

As it turned out, Beth McKendrick hadn't known him as well as she'd thought either, but she was still probably the one who knew him best. And if he hadn't loved her as she'd hoped, she was probably the one who loved him best. The pain of losing him had never faded. Partly because she'd never talked about it to anyone. A little to her father—not, even at the time, going so far as to share the depth of her grieving—and not at all to anyone else. Someone with a more critical self-awareness might have been struck by the similarities between Patrick's life and hers—the secrets, the internalizing—but Beth had never put herself, her own feelings, under the microscope. Perhaps because of that, she hadn't the tools to manage them when they ran out of control.

They were running out of control again now. She looked at the haunted face of Nicky Horn and wondered at the volume of hatred her heart could hold. Her voice shook with it. "Someone told you he loved you. And you called him a freak."

"I'm not proud of it," mumbled Horn, still avoiding the knives of her gaze.

"Well, that's something, I suppose," she managed. "The man I loved put his heart and soul into your hands. And you tore them into shreds and threw away the pieces. How could you do that? Whatever else he was, he was your friend, and he found the courage to be honest with you. And you treated him as if he'd done something shameful. You knew him, you knew how easy it was to hurt him—you must have known what that would do to him!"

"You're not watching the monitors."

"It wasn't like that," Horn protested weakly. "He didn't give me a chance. I needed time to get my head round it."

But Beth in her prescience was following the unfolding scene where he would not tell or have her see. Her mouth rounded in a slow *O*. "But there was no time. No *afterwards*, when you'd both calmed down enough to talk about it sensibly. As soon as the sun was up you were back out on the mountain, with the worst pitch of the climb ahead of you. If the storm had eased up at all, it certainly wasn't over, and you should have stayed in the tent. But you couldn't, could you? Not after what had happened. You wanted to finish the climb and put it behind you. And Patrick thought he'd lost you forever. On top of that he thought that, when you got back, you'd tell everyone. He thought his father would find out."

"I wouldn't have," insisted Horn, white-faced. "If he'd only given me more time. I could have dealt with it, if I'd just had a bit more time . . ."

"But you didn't say that, did you? Nothing to reassure or comfort him. And when he fell—"

"No," he begged her, knowing what she was going to say.

"When he fell," she went on remorselessly, "you thought it wasn't an accident. *If he'd given me more time . . .* You thought he *wanted* to

die, up there on Anarchy Ridge, in the pristine tumult of the snow—and he wanted you to die with him."

"He fell," whispered Horn. "He lost his footing. It was an accident . . ."

"Was it?" She searched his tortured face, learning nothing. "I can see how you'd want to think it was an accident. But the horror that stalks your nightmares is that Patrick Hanratty threw himself off Anarchy Ridge and tried to take you with him, because of what you did to him."

"You're not watching the monitors. *Look at the goddamned monitors!*"

Beth blinked and looked around her uncertainly as if she hadn't realized they were no longer alone.

McKendrick was halfway down the stone steps, leaning over the iron rail. His face was dark with fury and he was stabbing a finger at the bank of screens. "I give you one job to do. One simple job—watch the monitors, call me if anything happens. And you're so wrapped up in your own pathetic little melodrama you can't even do that!"

In the moment before Beth understood that her father wasn't shouting at her, her eyes filled with tears. It was as if she was losing everything—first Patrick, now Mack—as if neither of them had ever cared for her as she'd needed to be cared for, as she'd cared for them. She ached to be held, not shouted at. She'd never felt so lonely in her life.

Nicky Horn said, "I'm sorry, I—we . . ." His voice petered out as he took in what McKendrick was showing him.

Two of the screens were already blank. A third view of the grounds broke up even as he stared at it.

"He's taking them out," snarled McKendrick, though by then the others had caught up with him. "One by one, he's taking them off-line."

He grabbed Horn by the shoulder and hauled him bodily out of the way, dropping into the chair in his place. His long, strong fingers played urgently over the console, calling up other views. A lot of them were blank too.

Quick as it was in normal circumstances, most of Beth's mind was caught in another place. "Is it a power problem . . . ?"

"Yes, it's a power problem," snarled McKendrick. "He's finding the cameras one by one and cutting the power to them."

"I thought they were protected."

"They *are* protected. But not against someone like him. As our friend here keeps telling us, this is a professional."

And like a professional, he'd come equipped with a tool for every task. A moment before the next camera blanked, they actually saw him use the correct tool for neutralizing security cameras set high on unscalable walls.

"A slingshot?" exclaimed Horn. "A kid's slingshot?"

But it wasn't a child's toy, though the man could have passed it off as a present for a young nephew if it had been found in his possession. It had a pistol grip of carbon fiber and yellow power-bands that owed nothing whatever to Granny's knicker elastic, and it fired ball bearings that flew like bullets. Not the kind of slingshot to make little girls cry on school playgrounds—more the giant-killing kind. The steel projectile didn't just break the tempered glass at the front of the camera, it trashed the delicate mechanism behind. A split second after they saw him take aim, the picture went black.

"Answers one question," muttered Horn unsteadily, shaken

not even so much by this development as at the specters Beth had raised. "He hasn't gone home."

McKendrick snapped like an overstrained hawser, the recoil threatening to take off limbs and heads. He was out of the chair in one fast, fluid movement, and one of those long-fingered hands that somehow wasn't as soft as a pen pusher's should have been gripped the front of Horn's clothes, lifted him onto his toes, and slammed him back against the stone wall hard enough to drive the air from his lungs.

"You worthless piece of trash," McKendrick yelled into his startled face, "you think this is funny? You bring a killer to my door, and you think it's something to joke about?" The fist that wasn't pinning Horn to the wall backhanded him across the mouth, spraying blood. "Laugh at that. Go on, let's hear you. Laugh at that." He struck again, and then again. "Who the hell do you think you're dealing with? I buy and sell people like you every day!" He hit Horn once more, for luck.

"Mack. Mack!" Beth was dragging on his sleeve like a child. Except that she wasn't: she was using all her strength to try to restrain him. But all her strength was no match for all of his. "Please! That's enough."

Time flies when you're having fun. McKendrick hadn't been counting, but if he'd been asked to guess, he'd have said maybe he slapped Horn two or three times over six or seven seconds. When Beth's urgent demands recalled him to himself, he found that somehow rather more time, and rather more fists, had flown than he'd realized. Horn was hanging almost unconscious from his left hand. Blood from his mouth and nose covered Horn's shirtfront, and McKendrick's hand to the wrist, and spattered the monitors and the floor. When—days from now, perhaps even weeks—the police came looking for them, they'd assume the massacre started here, in the hall. And in a way they'd be right.

McKendrick hadn't meant to beat the younger man senseless, but he was a long way from forgiving him, even after the rage had passed. He opened his fist and watched with cold dislike as Horn slid down the wall, his strong young limbs rubbery, his wits scattered.

Beth hadn't forgiven him either, and she had more of a grudge to hold. But it's easier to hate someone you've never met, whose secrets you've never heard, than someone you've watched taking a hammering and choosing not to fight back. Horn didn't see the first blow coming, she thought, and toward the end he was incapable of fending them off, much less returning them. But in between there was half a minute where he stood and took it, his own fists hanging loose at his sides, making no attempt to defend himself. For all the world, thought Beth, as if he'd been waiting four years for this; as if through all his despair he'd clung to the hope that somebody beating the crap out of him for what had happened would somehow make it easier to bear.

Shocked by the violence—it's one thing to hear of men beating one another witless, quite another to witness it—and the whirlpool of her own feelings, she stood staring down at Horn, her lips parted as if on a question, waiting for him to move. To get up, to say something, to ask for help—*anything*. When he didn't, wordlessly she turned and went into the kitchen.

She returned with a wet cloth. First she dropped it on his chest. But he made no attempt to do anything with it, so after a moment she took it back and, bending, cleaned the worst of the blood from his face. Then she tipped his head forward and laid the cold wet of it on the back of his neck.

When she straightened up, his eyes were watching her.

McKendrick turned his back on Horn as something beneath contempt, transferring his attention—belatedly, it could be argued—to the monitors. Most of them were now reporting nothing. Such pictures as remained were scenic postcard shots of pleasant terraces and rolling acres. Perhaps the visitor hadn't been able to reach the cameras, or perhaps he hadn't seen much need to.

"We've lost our edge," said McKendrick tightly.

"Not much of an edge," ventured Beth. She was walking on eggshells. She'd never seen her father roused to such fury, was wary of provoking a fresh outburst. "The only time we saw him was as he shot out that camera."

It was true, but it wasn't much comfort. "So if he could avoid being seen till now, why do the cameras suddenly matter? What's he about to do that's different?"

There was only one possible answer, "He's going to try to come in here," said Beth.

"Right." McKendrick's glance was glacial. As if, at least for this moment, how he felt about Horn was how he felt about her too. "And while he was planning how and where and when, the two people who were supposed to be looking out for him, who were entrusted with all our lives, were arguing about which of them was a dead mountaineer's best bitch!" Nothing in his tone, or his face or his eyes suggested he found a kind of black humor in the situation. Beth knew that he was deathly serious. And he still had Nicky Horn's blood on his knuckles.

She swallowed nervously. "What do you want to do?"

144

McKendrick returned his attention to the screens and didn't favor her with a look again. "I don't see we have much choice. We defend ourselves as best we can."

"We can still give him up," she ventured. "If it really is him or us. No one would blame us."

McKendrick glanced scornfully at Horn, then his gaze came back in a double take. Until that moment he hadn't realized how much damage he'd done. Or that he had thereby limited their options, already narrow, even further. "Like that? You still think he can make a run for it? Beth, he'd need a head start of about half a day. Even then he might not get past the bottom of the garden."

"Maybe how far he gets isn't the important thing. Maybe the important thing is whether the man outside keeps trying to get inside after he's got what he came for."

"And maybe," said Nicky Horn through clenched teeth, "you should stop talking about me as if I was dead already."

Beth looked at him almost as if she were seeing him clearly for the first time. However much it might have suited her to think otherwise, he wasn't a monster. He'd made mistakes, he'd told lies. He'd been stupid and naïve. But the fact was, whichever of them cut the rope, Patrick Hanratty would not be alive today whatever Nicky Horn had or hadn't done. It was a waste of time and effort to go on hating him when mere pointed dislike was all he was worth.

She eyed him speculatively. In an odd way, giving up the hatred freed her to think more clearly. To focus on the priorities. "You know something, Horn? This is your lucky day. You had your shot at being a hero and you blew it. Now you can have something most people never get—a second chance. You can save my life, and Mack's, and Uncle William's. All you have to do is what you should have done, and know you should have done, and probably wish you'd done, four years ago."

"Is that what you want?" he asked, hollow-eyed. "If it is, I'll do it."

"Yes," said Beth.

"No," said McKendrick.

Almost, Horn seemed more tired than anything. He was weak and dazed from the beating, he was afraid of the man outside, and talking about what had happened on Anarchy Ridge had reopened wounds he'd thought half healed. But the tiredness was more disabling than any of that. A man could die of such tiredness. "Make your minds up," he said. "Let me know when you have."

The fanatic glint was back in McKendrick's eye, the iron in his voice. "You want to die for what you did? You think that'll even the score? Tough. I didn't bring you here to die. You've had four years to get yourself killed, and you couldn't manage it even with someone trying hard to help you. Now you're in my house and you'll play by my rules. Dying is the easy option. I've something else in mind for you. After it's done, you can die if you want to. But right now you'll fight for your life as if it was something of value, because you may be the only thing standing between my daughter and a man who'd kill her to protect his reputation. Is that clear? You belong to me. You'll do what I tell you to do."

McKendrick swiveled in his chair, brought Beth within the quadrant of his attack. "That goes for you too. I don't want to hear any more about Patrick Hanratty—who loved him, who he loved, whether he jumped off Anarchy Ridge or was pushed. I don't care. Do you understand? I don't care. All I care about is getting us through this. All of us. Because whether you like it or not, Horn's fate now is tied up with ours. Right now he needs me; soon enough

I'll need him. You don't need to know why. You *do* need to know that this is how it's going to be, and we're not having this argument again. Now go find yourself something to fight with. We're not going out with a whimper. If I've anything to do with it, we're not even going out with a bang."

Beth looked at him as if she didn't know him, as if they'd never met. But she didn't argue. She nodded and headed up the stairs toward the Great Hall and the rusty pile of historical armaments Horn had amassed.

Before she returned—with some kind of a halberd, waving it gingerly as if trying to work out how to use it—in his mind McKendrick had moved on to the next thing. "The walls, the doors, the shutters—that's our first line of defense. That's what'll hold him back longest. Killing the cameras was so that we wouldn't see where he's going to make his assault. He knows it'll take time and he doesn't want us getting ready for him. But he's figured out where our weak spot is and he's going to start hitting it."

"How long have we got?"

McKendrick shrugged. "If we left a window open, he's probably on the stairs now. If he's going to undermine a corner, it'll be days. Anything else, somewhere in between. I wish we could see. If we could see where he is—or even where he isn't—we could make an educated guess."

"What about the surviving cameras?"

"They tell us he isn't picking rosemary in the kitchen garden, he isn't practicing croquet on the lawn, and he isn't polishing the kitchen doorstep. That's all they tell us."

"Listen," said Horn.

They both listened. Beth shook her head. "I can't hear anything."

Horn still couldn't look at her. "No, *listen*. We can't see what he's up to, but we'll hear if he starts trying to dismantle a castle. Put your ear to the stonework and listen. He might be able to get in here unseen. He won't be able to do it in silence."

McKendrick nodded. "Yes. Good. Beth, you're the quickest. Well"—a hint of apology crept into his gaze—"right now you are. You take the upstairs. Set up a patrol route and listen at every wall, every window, for half a minute. Then on to the next. I'll do the same down here. Hell, I'd better go down into the cellars too—who knows what he has in mind? But this building was built to keep people out, and the shutters actually came with a guarantee. We'll get some warning. Once we know where he's coming in, we can figure out where to fight, and where to retreat."

Beth was looking at the bare stones. "Nobody's coming through there!"

"There isn't a prison in the world that's never been broken out of," said McKendrick shortly. "If you can break out of a prison, you can break into a fortress. And this is only a very small fortress. We need to be ready."

Convinced or not, she deferred to his authority. "All right. I'll do the Great Hall, the bedrooms, the roofs." She picked up the phones again. "And I'll keep trying these. We may still get lucky."

"That's the spirit," said McKendrick, but not as if he had much faith in it.

When she was gone, Horn put a hand out. McKendrick ignored it, turning his back. Horn sighed. "You can leave me here on the floor. Or you can help me up so I can listen at the kitchen door. Your choice."

McKendrick wanted to leave him where he was, bleeding on

the floor. But common sense prevailed. He gripped Horn's wrist and hauled him to his feet, and the way the younger man's breath hissed in his teeth was some recompense.

He steered Horn into the kitchen, hooked up a chair with his toe, located him against the wall between the back door and the shuttered window. "Call me if you hear anything. You shouldn't— he'd have taken out the courtyard camera if he was going to be working out there."

But it was the only job Horn was currently capable of, so he listened assiduously at the kitchen wall. He heard nothing. McKendrick did a circuit of the rest of the ground floor, and down into the basement, with the same result. He orbited through the kitchen at regular intervals, like a long-period comet.

About the third time he passed through, Horn said quietly, "I wasn't lying, you know. About Patrick. About how he fell."

McKendrick's jaw hardened. "I said I didn't want to hear any more about Patrick Hanratty. Not from Beth, and not from you."

"I know you did. But I'm not your daughter, and I'm not in your will. I don't see much need to do what you say."

"You need me to remind you?"

"You want to hit me again," sighed Horn, "go right ahead. Beating one another stupid will improve our chances enormously."

McKendrick, crossing the kitchen, paused to regard him coldly. "Maybe later. In the meantime, try to get your head round the fact that I don't care what happened to Patrick. He wasn't my friend, and I didn't want his babies. I don't care if he killed himself to save you, or you killed him to save yourself, or it really was an accident. Get that? I don't care. Now, can we drop it?"

"You seemed to care," said Horn, ignoring that. "When I told you I hadn't done what everyone thinks I did, it seemed to matter to you. You were shocked. *That* was the bit that shocked you!"

"Don't be absurd."

"I saw your face. Whatever it is you want me to do, that I could go to jail for, you thought it needed a man who'd cut his friend loose on a mountain. If that isn't what happened, you weren't sure I'd serve your purpose."

"I must have hit you once too often." McKendrick sniffed offhandedly. "Or not quite often enough." He headed back toward the hall.

Next time he passed through Horn said, "I know what you want me to do."

McKendrick broke his stride, turned and looked at him. Then he shook his head. "No, you don't. You don't need to know. When you need to know, I'll tell you."

But Horn wasn't being fobbed off again. While he'd nothing better to do than hold his ear against a wall he'd been thinking, and he'd finally made sense of everything McKendrick had done, everything he'd said. And he didn't want to say it aloud, and not only because he expected McKendrick would get his fists out once more. But he'd agreed in principle to something that, if he'd had more detail, or less need, he would never have countenanced. If he was going to die here today, he didn't want to do it with that agreement still in place.

He said, "You want me to kill someone for you. And I told you I wouldn't do that. I don't care what you did or tried to do for me, I won't do that for you."

It was hard to read McKendrick's expression. Partly because he was still angry with Horn, but also because of the ambivalence in it. Horn saw, or thought he saw, outrage in his face, and also amusement, which is a hard combination to carry off. McKendrick's head tilted quizzically to one side. "Who on earth do you suppose I want you to kill?"

Horn gritted his teeth, ready for the blow. "You want me to kill your brother William."

CHAPTER 11

MCKENDRICK DIDN'T HIT HIM, although for a moment it seemed a close-run thing. He stared at Horn as if he couldn't believe what he was hearing. "I love my brother."

"I know you do. That's why you want me to kill him. Because his life is pretty well intolerable, and he could live another ten years like this. Because you think the kindest thing you can do for him now is put an end to his suffering. And you don't want to do it yourself—you're not sure you *could* do it yourself, but if you could, you don't want to go to prison for it. Better to get someone else to do it. Someone who owes you a favor."

McKendrick was still standing over him, close enough to knock him from the chair with one swing that would arrive too fast for him to see it coming. The requisite tension was in his shoulders. But his arms stayed at his sides. "Is that what you think?"

"Yes."

"Anything else?"

"I think, if it still matters after today, you'll need to find someone else."

McKendrick gave a chilly smile. "Because you're coy about ending the misery of a helpless old man? You, who cut your best friend's rope! Patrick Hanratty, who was young and strong and didn't want to die, fell a thousand feet off Anarchy Ridge so you could come home safe. Don't you dare play the morality card."

"That's not what happened. I told you."

"You told me a pack of lies."

"No."

"You told *somebody* a pack of lies."

Horn couldn't argue with that. "I told you the truth."

McKendrick shook his head. "No. It happened the way you told the authorities it happened. At that point you didn't see any need to lie. You thought everyone would agree that you were right to cut the rope. You couldn't save Patrick, but you could stop him killing you. I can respect that. It's not very attractive, but I can respect it. But this other thing—*Patrick cut the rope because he loved me*— that's harder to forgive. That's scraping the bottom of a pretty murky barrel. Have the guts to be true to who you are. You're young and strong, and you haven't much time for weakness. You're pragmatic— you have to be to take on a mountain, the idea may be romantic but the reality is sheer bloody slog punctuated by moments of terror. And thoughts, and intentions, and *caring*, don't matter a damn to a mountain. Either you're strong and focused and practical or you die. That's who you are. And that's why I need you."

"I won't kill your brother," Nicky Horn repeated stubbornly. "However honorable your intentions, I won't do it."

"I didn't ask you to."

Horn's broken lips twisted in a sneer. "Then what the hell are we talking about? The win-win situation? Of course that's what you want. If you do it, you go to jail, and you've way too much to lose. If I do it, I still go to jail, but I won't be an old man when I come out. And you're not going to ask Beth, are you? You needed someone tough enough to do it, with no reputation left to lose, and desperate enough to take the deal. You must have thought it was your birthday when you found me.

"Which means there was nothing random about how we met. You didn't just happen to be passing, and you don't visit a prostitute in the area. You were looking for me too. You knew the story—of course you did, your daughter knew Patrick, that was reason enough for you to remember what happened in Alaska. And when you found you needed a ruthless bastard, to think of me."

Horn gave a desperate little snort that almost sounded like mirth. "I knew I'd got careless—I didn't realize I'd been careless enough for *two* hounds to pick up my trail. Of course, you can afford good help—as good as Tommy Hanratty's, I expect.

"And when he found me, he let you know, and you drove sixty miles to see me. I spotted you outside the café earlier. What were you waiting for? Did you think your proposition would sound better in daylight?

"Before that, though, fate stepped in. The *other* hound found me too. You saw what was happening and realized if you waited any longer I wasn't going to be any use to you. That's why you were willing to face down a gunman—you had a lot depending on it. And you didn't think you were going to be shot down in the street. People like you never do. You think you're too important to die." Horn grinned like a cornered wolf snarling. "Maybe you should take up climbing."

"Maybe you should *stick* to climbing," said McKendrick

sharply, "and leave philosophy to those better qualified. I don't want you to kill William. I've no way of knowing if his life still has any meaning for him or not, but I'm not taking a decision that important for him. He never asked me to hasten his death if he became too ill to do it himself. We never discussed it. If we had, if I was sure it was what he wanted, I'd do it myself and damn the consequences. Not because he's a burden to me, but because he's my brother and I love him and I'd do pretty much anything I could to help him, whatever the cost. I sure as hell wouldn't ask a self-obsessed little coward to do it for me."

Horn blinked. Not so much at the words—he'd heard worse, even in the privacy of his own head—but because he'd been sure he was right. All the pieces stacked up. The favor he'd promised to do without knowing what it was, that might cost him a spell in jail but only if the law caught up with him. The fact that McKendrick wouldn't talk in front of his daughter. When McKendrick knew that the time had come, that the job couldn't be put off any longer, he'd contact Horn—and Horn would do it because he wasn't sentimental, was he, he'd dropped his best friend off a mountain rather than risk falling with him. The world and its dog knew that Anarchy Horn would do just about anything if he thought it was in his own best interests. And promising a favor—any favor—to someone in a position to save his life would qualify. No wonder McKendrick had seemed thrown for those few minutes when he believed that Patrick had cut his own rope. If Horn hadn't killed his friend when the need was so pressing, the arguments so clear, there was no reason to hope he'd kill anyone else and McKendrick's plan would fail.

But there was no mistaking that stunned contempt in McKendrick's eyes and in his voice. A lot of things can be feigned, but

Horn didn't believe anyone was that good an actor. He'd seen contempt in people's eyes before, he knew what it looked like. "I—I'm sorry," he stumbled. "I thought . . . I'm sorry."

"So I should bloody well think," grunted McKendrick. He sounded almost breathless, as if the very idea had knocked the wind out of him.

"Then . . . what *is* it you want me to do? You might as well tell me. We're neither of us going to live long enough for it to be of more than academic interest."

McKendrick considered. He still hadn't forgiven Horn. "That sounds like a good reason for *not* telling you."

Horn shrugged. "Your choice. But if you can't or won't talk to Beth about it, and you do want to get it off your chest, I'm your only option. At least if you tell me, you know I'm not going to tell anyone else. If I did, they wouldn't believe me."

McKendrick's eyebrows climbed. "You think I need someone to hear my confession? And that, if I did, I'd choose you?"

"They say everyone needs someone to hear their confessions. It's what most people have friends for. Actually, it's not true. I haven't had a friend since Patrick. You can manage without. I think you're a man without many friends as well. Not the kind of friends you can share your darkest fears and secrets with. I'm not your friend either, but we seem to be in this together." Horn sniffed sourly. "If I got it wrong about William, at least I was right about you looking for me. Wasn't I?"

McKendrick looked away as if he deemed Horn unworthy of attention. "I don't owe you an explanation."

"No? You saved my life last night. And I thought it was incredible that a man would do that for someone he didn't even know.

Only you *did* know me, didn't you? At least by repute. And you had a job for me, something important enough to be worth the cost of tracking me down, and the potentially greater cost of hanging on to me. Yes, I'm pretty sure you owe me an explanation."

"Don't flatter yourself," sneered McKendrick. "There's nothing special about you, except that I knew enough about you to recognize the qualities I was looking for: youth, self-importance, and no morals. But that's nothing to be proud of. The best that can be said of you is that you can't help being young."

But Horn was pretty sure this was his last chance to know what he was doing here and wouldn't be put off. "You chose me for this job because you thought I killed Patrick. That's what you want to believe—it suits you for me to be that man. Anyone else would be glad to think that Patrick Hanratty took the decision for himself, but you weren't. You were horrified. Why? If you don't need my help with William, what is it you want me to do that only a man with no morals would agree to?"

McKendrick smiled. He'd locked the anger away, and with it any chance that he might—inadvertently or in spite—say more than he wanted to. He was back in control, of himself if not the situation. "You're wrong," he said, "and so are *they*. I have plenty of friends, and I don't need anyone to confess to. See this?" A glance around the kitchen encompassed by implication the whole castle and more. "I made this." He didn't mean he built it stone by stone. "My father was a farmer. He called himself a gentleman farmer, but that just meant he was better at opening fêtes than milking cows, and he ended up having to sell the land to pay his debts. He was bankrupt and an invalid by the time he was sixty.

"What I have, I made from scratch." McKendrick said it with

a pride so adamant you could break your knuckles on it. "And I didn't do it by cultivating other people's opinions. I need someone to pour my heart out to like a seal needs roller skates. I've taken my own decisions since I was fifteen years old. I don't need someone to bounce them off, or talk them through with, and I certainly don't need anyone to advise me. And if by any chance I did, I could do so much better than you.

"All you need to know—all you're *going* to know—is that I have a use for you. When I'm ready, I'll tell you what I expect you to do. If one or both of us dies first, you're off the hook. Otherwise, you'll do what I tell you."

And Nicky Horn thought there was nothing more he could do, nothing more he could say, to get at the truth. He thought he was going to die in ignorance. Robert McKendrick was like a man carved from marble: shiny, hard and impervious. A man quite capable of carrying his secrets to the grave if he chose to. There was no pressure Horn could exert to make him change his mind.

Perhaps it was in becoming a self-made man that he'd tempered such a degree of mental toughness. But probably he had the attitude first, and it was that which made it possible for him to succeed. Horn was the one who did battle with mountains. But he no longer kidded himself he was as tough as McKendrick.

He gave it one last try. "You haven't told Beth, either, have you? Why not? Because you know she won't approve? That she'd try to stop you?"

McKendrick's expression slammed shut almost audibly, like a vault door. "Leave Beth out of this. It has nothing to do with her."

"It's why someone wants to break into her house and wipe out her family! Maybe you don't owe me one, but you sure as hell owe her an explanation. She deserves to know what she's going to die for."

The way McKendrick rounded on him, Horn thought he was going to be hit again. He flinched involuntarily. But the only missiles McKendrick let fly were words. "I don't want to hear my daughter's name on your lips again. She is none of your business. You've hurt her too much already. I hurt her too, bringing you here. I didn't know how much, and anyway it needed doing, but from now on you keep away from her. I'll look after Beth. All you have to do is keep your mouth shut and do what you're damn well told."

Horn's eyes had slipped out of focus as he replayed their conversations, this one and the earlier ones, the way he replayed climbs he'd made, seeing every tortuous step, every killing inch, in his mind's eye.

McKendrick thought he'd finally battered Horn into silence and thanked God for it. If Horn had kept picking away at him, sooner or later he'd have said too much—enough for Horn to put it together. His wild surmising had already brought him too close for comfort. McKendrick didn't want, by words said or unsaid, by a gesture or a look, to let Horn know where he'd been near and where wide of the mark.

McKendrick resumed his patrol of the ground floor, between the front door, the monitors, the sitting room, and the kitchen door. He went down into the undercroft and listened at the bare stone walls. He heard nothing. He was only a little reassured.

The third time he passed through the kitchen, Horn said, "How did your father die?"

McKendrick froze in his tracks. It might have been a lucky

shot, it might have been nothing of the kind. "What?" His voice was choked with evasion.

"It's a simple enough question. You said he died bankrupt and an invalid. So what did he die of?"

"Old age."

"Really? Because these days, lots of people your age still have their parents around. How old was he when he died?"

McKendrick didn't have to answer. Somehow, he felt he did. "Seventy-three."

"But he was an invalid by the time he was sixty."

McKendrick said nothing.

"What about your mother? Is she dead too?"

Briefly McKendrick shut his eyes. "Yes."

Horn gave it a little more thought. Finally he said, "And William's been ill for years. It's the Alzheimer's, isn't it—it's like a family curse. Both your parents had it, and your older brother has it. And you're afraid it's going to happen to you too. Maybe you know it is—maybe you can feel it happening.

"That's what you can't tell Beth, and what you sure as hell can't ask for her help with. You don't want to go the way your parents went, the way William's going—dying by inches. That scares you more than anything on earth. More than a gunman in the street, even more than one at your door.

"But there is a way out, for someone determined enough to meet the problem head-on. William never asked for your help, and maybe that was because he didn't want it, but maybe it was for the same reason you won't ask Beth—he didn't want you to ruin your life rescuing him from his. For that you need someone you don't care about. Someone you have a hold over, and someone with nothing to lose.

"What would you have done if Hanratty's man *hadn't* caught up with me just then? It was the perfect opportunity to put me in your debt—it could have been a while before you found another one as good. That's why you were watching me. To find something I needed that you could provide, so when the time came I'd provide something you needed.

"It isn't William's life you want me to finish off, is it?" Nicky Horn's voice was thin as paper. As if he were staring into an abyss. "When things get too hard—when the brain cells start to die, and first of all you can't run a financial empire anymore, then you can't keep the household accounts, *then* you can't add two and two without using your fingers—you want to be able to pick up the phone and say, 'It's time,' and have me come and put an end to yours."

CHAPTER 12

HE COULDN'T BELIEVE what he was saying. All the same, he knew this time he'd got it right. Even he wasn't sick enough to have dreamed it up if the clues weren't there, if the tap-tap-tapping in his brain wasn't the explanation trying to get itself heard.

But he expected McKendrick to deny it. The man volunteered nothing. He'd gone to considerable lengths, and no small amount of risk, to get his way on this, and to get it without anyone else knowing what he had in mind.

Robert McKendrick was a powerful man. He'd been a successful and powerful man in a cutthroat business for so long that it informed all his dealings, defined the very shape that he occupied in the world. Part of it was that he lied all the time. He told business competitors that he wanted things that he didn't want, and had things that he didn't have, and wasn't interested in things he'd have sold his granny to get hold of. It was like a great game of charades, only without the rules. He thought nothing of lying—not when it was him doing it, not when it was a rival. It was how the game was played.

But that was when the other players were also successful and powerful men. He never lied to underlings, people of no consequence. He would have deemed it beneath him. He met Horn's stare of god-forsaken shock and said, "Yes." Quite calmly. Not as if he was saying something that should have shook the heavens.

"No!" exclaimed Horn.

"I assure you," said McKendrick solemnly, "you've finally got there. It may have taken you all morning, you may have gone all round the houses first, but you've finally got it right. William may not have thought far enough ahead to know what was going to happen to him and take steps to deal with it, but I did. I found you."

"I mean, no," stumbled Horn. "I won't do it."

McKendrick elevated an eyebrow at him. "You've already agreed. A contract exists."

"I didn't know *then*!"

"You knew what *you* were getting out of it. Your life—which, may I remind you, was entirely uninsurable at the point at which I stepped in. Was there anything you *wouldn't* have given for it right then?"

"No. Yes! I don't know. But I told you—I *told* you—I wouldn't hurt anyone."

"No one's going to be hurt. I told *you*, it's a victimless crime."

"You want me to *kill* you! To put you to sleep, like an old dog that keeps peeing on the rug!"

"But I can't be the victim if it's my choice!" Then the exasperation melted out of his voice and McKendrick sighed. "Nicky, you're a young man. When I was your age, I was afraid of death as well. I know better now. I saw my father reduced to a helpless shell. I saw the terror in his eyes. It never left him. Long after he'd forgotten who I was, after he'd forgotten who *he* was, he knew absolutely the horror of what was happening to him.

"People say that Alzheimer's is harder on the family than on the patient." McKendrick shook his head. "Don't you believe it. My father suffered every day. He was frightened every day. He imagined things that weren't real, terrible things—that people were hurting him, plotting against him. It was impossible to comfort him. When all his memories had gone, when his ability to reason was gone, he still believed the increasingly bizarre outpourings of his dissolving brain.

"Of course he did. What choice did he have? Our whole lives depend on our ability to distinguish between what's real and what's not. We believe what we see and hear and can reasonably deduce. Things that we dream, or imagine, may seem real at the time but we can recognize the difference. You might dream about having a terrible argument with someone, but you don't stay mad at them after you've woken up. Dreams get filed in a different part of your brain. A healthy brain doesn't mix them up."

He paused for a moment, organizing his thoughts. Marshaling his argument. "But the system depends on the brain functioning properly. Reporting accurately. Collecting the messages that come in from the senses and processing the information in a rational way.

"With dementia, gaps start appearing where previously there were connections. Things get lost or jumbled up. The brain screws up its filing system. It puts some things in the wrong file, and some things in the right file but with the wrong index card, and some things miss the drawer altogether and drop down the back of the cabinet. So when that knowledge is needed again, it may open the correct file but it's anybody's guess what's going to come out. It might be right. It might be nearly right. It might be absolute nonsense, but we go on believing the information in the filing cabinet because we have no choice. Inside ourselves, the brain is the only arbiter of what's what. There is no fallback position, no referee.

"It's like . . ." McKendrick hunted round for an analogy, something to explain the ineffable. Instinct guided him to one that might make sense to Horn. "It's like you're standing on a frozen lake. The lake has always been frozen and the ice has always been strong. But now as you stand on it, it starts to crack. At first it's just thin little lines that shoot out from under your feet. But then the cracks grow bigger, and the ice begins to groan, and the water starts seeping through. And you know what's going to happen: it's going to break up and throw you into the freezing lake and you're going to die. But—and this is the biggie, this is the killer—*there's nowhere else to stand.* As your brain changes, your perception of reality changes with it. Everything you know, everything you've ever known, is telling you that it's the rest of the world that's gone mad.

"So my father *knew* that people were hurting him. He knew that I was stealing all his money, and William wanted—you'll like this—William wanted to sell him to white slavers. He'd have been about sixty-eight at this point. Nothing would persuade him of the inherent unlikelihood of it. And he never got it wrong—it was never William stealing his money and me selling him to the slavers. It wasn't something he'd invented to hurt us—in his own mind it was real. We employed nurses to care for him, and we made sure he couldn't wander off. He thought we'd imprisoned him. He lived the last decade of his life in fear and misery."

McKendrick stopped there, his face haunted, and Horn

thought he wouldn't be able to go on. But after a moment he sucked in a deep breath and composed himself. "That decade turned him from a healthy middle-aged man to something stick-thin under a sheet, his skin so fragile the bones were in danger of poking through. By then he'd lost his ability to speak, to feed himself, to sit up, even to swallow. All he had left was the horror. One evening when I was sitting with him, he breathed out and didn't breathe in again. I can honestly say I've never been gladder in my life.

"Mum was luckier. She was younger than Dad, and she'd been nursing him for three years when she felt the same thing starting in her. She knew what was coming. She tried to keep it from us, me and William, but that only worked while she was able to juggle, to use the faculties she still had a grip on to compensate for those that were slipping. But she didn't live long enough to deteriorate the way Dad did. She had a heart attack. When the paramedics opened her blouse to listen for a heartbeat, they found the words *Do not resuscitate* tattooed on her chest.

"Can you *imagine*..." His voice cracked and he had to try again. "Can you imagine the despair, the sense of utter desolation, that would lead a middle-class, middle-aged woman to have that done? The paramedics wondered if it was some kind of joke. But I knew she'd never been more serious about anything in her life."

He made himself smile, and a frail and naked thing it was. "With both parents smitten by early-onset Alzheimer's, it came as no surprise whatsoever when William started getting funny notions. At first they weren't so funny that they couldn't have been true. Someone kept moving his papers at work, he could never find what he needed. There was something wrong with his car, except it didn't do it when he took it to the mechanic. He found the new one-way system near his home unnecessarily complicated.

"Then one day he phoned me and said he'd got lost and would I come and find him? He'd been driving home from his office—I found him two streets over from where he'd lived for twelve years. It turned out there wasn't even a one-way system. I took him home and we both had a stiff drink, and then we talked about what was happening to him. We both knew what it was, of course, and that it was only going to get worse. He never drove the car again. He sold it the next day and set up a contract with a taxi firm.

"The day after that I took him to see his doctor. They have this damn fool test they do, where they ask you who the prime minister is and whether you can count backwards and stuff like that. And William was sailing through it. I was beginning to think we were wrong, it was something else—a virus, a tumor, something you could hope to cure. Then she asked him how old he was. And he said he was thirty-one. He knew his date of birth. He knew the current year. But when he was asked to subtract one from the other, he kept getting thirty-one. So she asked him to look in a mirror. Something he did every morning when he was shaving. And for a moment he didn't recognize himself. When he did, these enormous slow tears slid down his cheeks."

"And that's . . ." Horn cleared the scratch out of his throat and tried again. "And that's about ten years ago?"

"Getting on for. He managed to keep some sort of a life together at first. He took early retirement—told people he wanted to enjoy his garden while he was still fit enough to get out in it. We made sure that if he got lost, people would know to call his house.

He wasn't dangerous, even to himself. While he was still pretty much on top of things, he hired in all the help he needed. That worked well until the growing confusion started to outweigh the residual lucidity.

"By then he was dependent on someone for just about everything. And I wasn't happy leaving him with people I didn't know and couldn't supervise. There are plenty of well-qualified, professional, kind people out there who'd have done a good job of looking after him. But what if I got it wrong and left him with one of the other sort? The lazy sort, the greedy sort—even the vicious sort? Even if he'd have been able to tell me, would I have believed him? I needed to be on the spot. So I brought him here. About four years ago now."

They'd strayed a little off the point, but Horn never considered prompting him. This was the longest they'd talked, and it explained so much of what was going on, both in McKendrick's life and in his head.

His head . . .

"When . . ." Again the catch in Horn's throat tripped him. "When did you start getting symptoms?"

McKendrick laughed out loud, a savage sound. "Thanks, Nicky. I haven't yet. This is all me, genuine and unreconstructed. If you think I'm behaving irrationally, you should see me on a bad day."

From somewhere Horn pulled a little censorious frown. "I never know when you're joking."

"That's easy," said McKendrick briefly. "I never joke. I'm always in deadly earnest."

"And you want someone to kill you before you end up like William."

Something, some emotion, washed through McKendrick that for a moment he didn't recognize. But it was relief. At having it out it the open. At having it fixed and framed by words. The idea had lived in his head and nowhere else, growing but also festering, for over a year now. He'd guarded it like a treasure because he knew there was no one he could share it with for fear of being stopped. It had taken him two or three months to be sure this was what he wanted to do, and the rest of the time to find a way of doing it. That's a long time to keep a secret.

"Right now I could do it without any help at all. But right now it doesn't need doing. I enjoy my life—I don't want to cut the good bit short. But if I leave it until it needs doing, I won't be able to manage alone. I might not even recognize that the time has come. I'm going to need help. Someone who knows what needs doing and how to do it. Someone who knew me when I was rational enough to state unequivocally what I wanted."

McKendrick let out a slightly uneven breath and his eyes dipped momentarily closed. Someone knew. Someone knew, and now he could talk about it. "And it can't be Beth. I don't know if she'd do it; but if she did, she'd be prosecuted. However sympathetic a court might be, mercy killing still counts as murder—she could lose everything. That's why I need you. Of course I knew who you were, what you'd done—at least, what you said you'd done. I thought you were perfect for my purposes. Getting you on board was important enough to risk my own neck doing it." He gave a wry little smile. "Mind, knowing what you know now, you may feel that wasn't as big a gamble as it first appeared."

"You had people out looking for me?"

"Yes."

"How long?"

"Four months. They're top people, good at what they do. When they found you they let me know, but I didn't want them to approach you. I wanted to talk to you myself—to find out if you'd left Alaska sufficiently far behind that my proposition wouldn't interest you. When I saw a man with a gun shove you up a dark alley, I knew you hadn't."

Horn couldn't argue with that. "When were you going to tell me?"

"I *wasn't* going to tell you. I was going to offer you a job. You're a carpenter, aren't you? There's always work to be done in a place like this. Once I'd made contact with you, and you had somewhere to work and a place to live that you didn't have to leave in a hurry every few weeks, there'd have been time to get round to the other thing. As it turns out, we've been rather overtaken by events."

There wasn't much arguing with that, either. Horn was watching McKendrick's face intently. "So, if we come through this, I get a job as your handyman and a cottage in the grounds. And one day, maybe years from now, you ask to see me in your study, and it's not because you're giving me the sack, or even a pay rise. It's because your mind's going and you're scared you can't hold things together much longer, and you want to tell me how and when you want it done. To get hold of a gun and ambush you in the Lime Walk. Or some of that blue stuff they put horses down with, and inject you while you sleep." Horn looked him full in the face. "Is that what we're talking about?"

McKendrick considered the details a shade gothic, but Horn seemed to understand the wider picture pretty well. "Perhaps not a cottage in the grounds. At least, not until Beth's resigned to having you around. But I'll set you up somewhere not too far away. Somewhere I can protect you from Hanratty."

"What if I refuse?"

"Why would you refuse? You owe me your life. Why would you refuse me a favor that might cost you just a few years of it?"

"I don't know, Mr. McKendrick." The strain was audible, stretching Horn's voice. "Maybe, because it's wrong?"

"To rescue someone from fear and suffering? When that person has made it abundantly clear that it's what he wants, and has done from the day he realized it was going to become an issue? How can that be wrong?"

"Don't ask me," snarled Horn, "ask the Lord Chamberlain. *He* seems to think it's wrong!"

"No, he thinks it's illegal. That's different. I'll give you something in writing to produce if the police catch up with you. It won't keep you out of court, but it'll show that you weren't acting on your own authority. And that Beth didn't hire you to speed through her inheritance. Nicky, nobody will think you did anything very wicked. It's a bit of a gray area, I admit—they only call it assisted suicide if you have the physical strength and the mental clarity to do the final act yourself. But everyone except the law knows there's all the difference in the world between murder and mercy killing, and nobody apart from cranks thinks what I'm proposing is wrong anymore."

"What if *I* think it's wrong?"

McKendrick looked at Horn, as he sometimes did, as if he'd brought him in on the sole of his shoe. "It doesn't matter what you think. You owe me this. You don't have to like it. Anyway"—his narrow jaw rose combatively—"what entitles you to take the moral high ground? You cut your best friend's rope!"

Horn's voice was low. "I told you, that isn't what happened."

"You told the police something different. And you told Beth something else again. I think you've told so many lies even you aren't sure what the truth is anymore.

"I'll tell you what the truth is—the only truth that matters. Patrick Hanratty was on your rope, and now he's dead. His father blames you, and his father's hit man is just the other side of this wall. You don't have to like me—in fact, it's probably better if you don't. But by God, Nicky, if you want to live through today, you'd better start seeing things my way!"

"Because you'll shove me outside if I don't?" In the white face, Horn's eyes flamed with a kind of desperate rebellion.

"Maybe that's exactly what I'll do. It's what *you* did—bought your safety with someone else's life. It would be a kind of poetic justice."

They glared at one another across the little kitchen, both stoking the anger they hoped would protect them from fear. Their backs were against the wall. Even if Hanratty's man had got bored and gone home, their backs would still have been against the wall.

Horn broke the savage silence. "And what's Beth going to say when she hears about this?"

"Beth isn't *going* to hear about this," McKendrick shot back, "until you've paid your debt. After that she'll probably have to know. And yes, she'll hate you forever. She'll hate me too. I can live with that." He grinned a vivid acknowledgment of the irony. "I can't afford to worry too much about what Beth wants. I have to concentrate on what she needs. And this is it—this is the best I can do. And, God help me, I need your cooperation to do it."

"Then, Mr. McKendrick, you have a problem."

"You think this is easy for me?" When McKendrick's temper flared, suddenly Horn could see the likeness between him and his daughter. She didn't take after him physically. But her temperament—her intellectual arrogance, her risk-taking, her absolute single-mindedness—she'd inherited from him almost unchanged. "This isn't how I wanted my life to be! When I was your age, I was working like a maniac so I could enjoy the kind of lifestyle I wanted. For my family, but also for myself. I imagined that around now I'd be planning my retirement. A boat on the Med. Maybe a beach house in the Seychelles. Enough money amassed to provide for whatever I wanted, whatever opportunities came along.

"I did *not* imagine I'd be spending my time and money and, yes, risking my neck trying to persuade someone to do me the final kindness when playing out the hand I've been dealt has become unbearable. Because that's what we're talking about, Nicky. A life so frightening that no one should be made to live it. Don't have any illusions about what it is I'm facing. I'm not going to be just a charming old dodderer whose socks never match. I'm going to be a broken and tormented man who won't know a moment's peace short of death but who might have to wait ten or fifteen years for it."

McKendrick's voice was actually shaking. It was hard to avoid the conclusion that it was shaking with fear. He took a moment to steady it. "Look on the bright side. I might never get this illness. I might die of something else first, or I might live to be a hundred with my marbles perfectly intact. And that's something that would give me enormous satisfaction.

"But if I don't kill myself while I'm fully in command of my wits—if I wait until the symptoms start—I won't do it at all. Because by then I won't think it needs doing. I'll think everybody else is being thoroughly unreasonable if not downright cruel but I'm the same as I've always been. I need to have this all organized long before that. I need to set up some kind of chain of events—when Beth notices I'm starting to lose it, she tells my solicitor, and my solicitor posts a sealed letter he's never read and you get your instructions—while I can still work it all out. I can't leave it until it matters. Do you understand that?"

Horn nodded slowly. "I understand it. I just can't do what you want me to."

"You can," retorted McKendrick, no shadow of doubt in his voice, "and you will. It's the price of what I've done for you. What I'm still doing. If you live through today, it'll be down to me. So do what you're told, do your time, go away somewhere and get on with your life. I'll make sure there's money to help with that—help you go somewhere Hanratty can't follow.

"It's the best deal you're going to get, Nicky. You ought to grab it with both hands."

Incredibly, Horn seemed to be thinking about it. His voice wasn't much more than a whisper. "I don't think there is anywhere Hanratty can't follow. I *know* there's nowhere Patrick can't follow."

It wasn't that McKendrick very much cared about Nicky Horn's ghosts. It was more that he knew he needed to deal with them before Horn would be much use to him. "Tell me what happened. The truth, this time. I don't care what the truth is, I just want to hear it."

Horn sighed. It was a long time ago. And McKendrick was right, it really didn't matter anymore. Except that if he was going to die because of it, there wouldn't be another chance. If he wanted someone to bear witness for him, it had to be Robert McKendrick. "Patrick was leading. We shouldn't even have been climbing in those conditions, but we were. Three-quarters of the way up Anarchy Ridge, with the wind throwing bucketloads of snow in our faces, suddenly he wasn't there anymore and the rope went tight.

"What I told Beth, about what he'd said—what we both said—the night before: that's how it started. Now we were like strangers. I was angry with him, he was upset with me. When he went off the ridge, I didn't know if he'd fallen or jumped, if he wanted me to die there with him or not. I held on to him, swore to him I wouldn't let go. But after three hours I was exhausted, and I couldn't get him back, and I was shit-scared of falling with him. That's when he cut the rope. He fell, yelling my name." There were tears on Horn's face that McKendrick thought he was entirely unaware of.

"And that's the truth?"

Horn nodded. His eyes were hollow, whether with fear or remembrance McKendrick couldn't judge. "No point lying now."

"There never was much point. You lied rather than tell his family that Patrick was in love with you, and you rejected him, and you'll always be afraid that's why he died. But if you'd told them the truth, it's hard to see how things could have worked out any worse."

"They didn't take it as well as I'd hoped," admitted Horn.

"Maybe not." McKendrick's scrutiny seemed to flay Horn's soul. "Or maybe you wanted them to hate you. Them, and everyone else. You thought you deserved it. You thought it was your fault Patrick was dead. You said you cut his rope because you couldn't bring yourself to say you broke his heart."

Horn's voice seemed to come from a long way off. "Yes."

"But Nicky—what if he just fell? What if it was just an accident? It was blowing a gale up there, there was snow everywhere, you couldn't tell where the rocks ended and the ice began. What if

Patrick just made a mistake? You were climbing an untried pitch in an Alaskan blizzard, for God's sake! I don't know much about climbing, but I know this much: everyone falls sometimes. The rock crumbles, the ice breaks away. And neither of you had your whole mind on the job. I don't think Patrick was trying to punish you. I think he was just unlucky."

"You weren't there," whispered Nicky Horn. "I'd give anything—anything—to believe that. But I don't. I can't. Five hours earlier he said he loved me, and I called him a freak. They were almost the last words we said to one another."

"You were taken by surprise."

"I didn't have to humiliate him! I didn't have to rip everything from him—our friendship, his dignity, everything. He thought he'd lost the lot. He thought I despised him. And I didn't! That was the first lie—the worst lie. I didn't feel the way he felt, but if it had been two other guys we'd been talking about I wouldn't have re-acted like that. I don't know why I said what I did. If we'd had one more day I could have told him—apologized, told him everything would be all right. We'd have finished the climb and gone home friends.

"Why did I do that?" By now the tears were falling openly, streaking Horn's face. He made no effort to dash them away. Mc-Kendrick thought that he genuinely wanted an answer. That it had taken him four years to even ask the question, and now he needed an answer. "Why would I tear him apart like that?"

"Because," said McKendrick with an uncharacteristic gentle-ness, "you're only human. You make mistakes too. It was just bad timing all round. If it had happened back in England, he'd have gone out to drown his sorrows, and after the hangover had worn off he'd have been working out what he needed to do to get his life back on track. It happens all the time: people we love turn out not to love us. You get over it.

"But it didn't happen in England. It happened on a mountain ridge in the middle of one of the world's great wildernesses, with a gale howling in his ears. And mountains do things to people, don't they? Beth's talked about it. You can see so far, you feel so small. . . . The sea's like that too. It sucks you in. People say they sail in order to leave their problems behind, but I don't think that's what it is. When you're out there like a flyspeck on the map, surrounded by nothing but the elements, your values change. Everything's either very, very close or very far away. It's hard to keep a sense of perspective.

"Yes, you handled it badly. But so did Patrick. He shouldn't have cornered you with this when there was nowhere for you to retreat. He should have known it could only end with at least one of you being hurt."

"We were days from civilization," Horn remembered. He was talking now almost as if he were asleep, a heartaching monotone. "I thought he couldn't face the long hike back. When you're climbing, your mind's full to bursting and you put the personal stuff on the back burner. But walking back, hour after hour, after he'd reached out to me and I'd bitten his hand off at the wrist . . . I thought he couldn't face it. I thought he'd decided stepping off into the white-out was a better option."

Against the habit of a lifetime, McKendrick found himself feeling what this young man had felt. Empathy. It's a terrible idea in business, to feel for the people you've just shafted. "Nicky, you're never going to know exactly what was going through Patrick's head. But you know he was a good man, and a good friend. You know he'd looked after you every other time you'd climbed together, as you'd looked after him. Even if he *was* hurt, even if he was upset, why would he suddenly turn into someone else? If he'd fallen twelve hours earlier, you wouldn't even have asked yourself if there was something more to it."

"I thought—I think—I thought I'd killed him. Was responsible for his death. As surely as if I *had* cut the rope." But if Horn couldn't decide on the tense, that meant he was no longer sure. He'd felt so guilty about Patrick Hanratty's death that he'd lied, and gone on lying even after he realized it could cost him his life. Now this tall man, this stranger, this cold man whose heart was a battlefield, was telling him he'd been mistaken. It was just an accident. Perhaps it was just an accident all along.

But if that was so . . . Horn shook his head. He couldn't begin to come to terms with what that meant. That he'd spent four years running, and was probably going to die, for nothing. It was almost better to go on believing what he'd always believed, that at least there was a kind of justice to it.

Watching the turmoil in the younger man's face, suddenly it occurred to McKendrick that they'd been talking about this for too long. That too long had passed since he'd checked the monitors or Horn had listened at the kitchen door. He turned abruptly and strode back into the hall.

Another of the screens had gone blank. It didn't matter. McKendrick could see where Hanratty's man was. He was standing in the courtyard, in full view of one of the three remaining cameras, waiting patiently for someone to notice him, and he was holding Beth McKendrick in front of him like a shield.

CHAPTER 13

HORN COULDN'T SEE the monitors from where he sat in the kitchen. And McKendrick didn't cry out or even gasp. Instead he locked down, willing his body to be still, freeing up all his energies, all his considerable mental acumen, to tackle this new challenge. To weigh up what it meant and work out how to deal with it.

But a stillness that absolute creates a kind of shock wave. It traveled out from the hall, and when it reached the kitchen Horn straightened up and listened, and after a moment he hauled himself to his feet and walked quietly through the sitting room. He couldn't have guessed what was meant by the almost concrete silence, but he knew it wasn't natural and he doubted it was good.

When he reached the hall, he could see what McKendrick could see. Immediately he knew exactly what it meant. Though his tone was tissue-thin, he managed to keep it steady. He was pleased about that. "So now you open the door."

McKendrick didn't answer. Perhaps he didn't hear. All his attention was focused on the monitor. "What the *hell* did she go outside for?"

"She didn't," said Horn. "He did what I said he'd do—he found a way inside."

McKendrick looked round at Horn as if he'd forgotten he was there. "Then why is he out there again and not in here?"

It was pretty obvious to Horn, but then his emotions weren't involved, or not in the same way. "Because we can't rush him down a camera cable. He can update us on the new situation without the risk that one or both of us will come over all heroic and take him on."

McKendrick looked the younger man up and down, taking in the old bruises and the new ones.

Horn felt himself flush under the scrutiny. "Yeah, well," he growled, "he doesn't know about that, does he? As far as he's aware, I'm pretty well back to fighting fitness. And you're in good shape for a middle-aged guy, *and* you're her father. Any animal will fight for its cub. He doesn't want to fight. He just wants to get the job done. Now he has."

McKendrick's face had drained to the color of old grate-ash. Behind that, though, the intellectual arrogance that had made him a rich man was wrestling with the shock. Deep in the marrow of his bones was a part of him that couldn't believe, that wouldn't believe, that he'd been outmaneuvered. "He thinks now he can have you without a fight. That I'll open the shutters and you'll walk meekly outside."

"Yes." Horn couldn't think of anything else to say.

"A straight trade. You for Beth."

"Yes."

"Will he honor it? When he has you, will he leave?"

The truth couldn't do him much good now. Whatever the ultimate outcome, McKendrick had no choice about what he did next. Horn said what the man needed to hear. "He might. If he can get me without a struggle, he might decide to quit while he's ahead. You'll call the police as soon as you can get to a phone that works, but he'll be miles away by then, with all middle England to vanish into."

McKendrick's eyes were coming back into focus. "Won't he be worried that I'll give the police his description?"

"He's a pro. He'll change how he looks. You could see him again, a week from now, crossing Waterloo Bridge with an umbrella under his arm, and you'd never recognize him. He knows that."

"That's not what you said before."

A moment's hesitation as Horn back-pedaled. "No." He gave a tiny grin. "I thought I had a better chance if your best interests were the same as my best interests."

"And now you don't?"

"I think my chances are all used up. But you may still have one, if you play your cards right. Dead right, first time."

McKendrick wanted to be absolutely sure that he understood what Horn was telling him. "You're saying I should hand you over and hope for the best."

"I don't think there's anything else you can do."

There was a pause while McKendrick almost seemed to wonder, to resist coming to the same conclusion. But he couldn't. He couldn't find an alternative because there wasn't one. "I can't let him hurt Beth. Not if there's any hope she can come safe through this."

"I'll . . ." Horn was going to say he'd get his things. One word into the sentence he realized there was no point. He wouldn't be doing any more carpentry. "Open the door. Shut it and lock it again as soon as I'm outside. If he can't see an easy way to get at you, I think he'll let Beth go. If he can't silence all the witnesses, he's better not killing any of them."

"Just you."

There was a world of tiredness, of acceptance, in Horn's pale smile. "I've stayed ahead of the game for four years. That's four years more than Patrick got. I think maybe it's enough."

Incredibly, McKendrick found a lump in his throat. "There has to be another way. How can I . . . ?"

Horn knew the answer to that. "Because you have to. You can find someone else to do . . . what you wanted me for. You can't find yourself another daughter."

"We could make a fight of it . . ."

"If we do that, we'll all die. He's not just the man with the gun, he's the one who knows what he's doing. How this works, how it pans out. Every time. And he has no conscience. That's more than an edge—it's a whole bloody sword. Even in a crisis, most people hesitate before they'll hurt someone else. He won't. He'll kill you like swatting a fly if you give him the ghost of a chance. So don't. Keep the castle locked down until you know he's gone. Don't even open the door to let Beth in. She's safe as long as you're safe." Probably, Horn added privately. He moved toward the door.

McKendrick put out a hand that stopped short of actually touching him. As if he were already out of reach. Then his fingers went to the console but again hesitated, as if he couldn't bring himself to touch it either.

"You have to open the door," Horn said again. It almost sounded as if he was pleading. As if dying was no longer the worst thing that he faced. "You have to let me go. Or he'll hurt her."

Eyes haunted by guilt, McKendrick tore his gaze away from

the young man's face and sought his daughter's on the monitor. The man was still standing behind her, showing little of himself besides his hands gripping her shoulders—firmly rather than tightly, no hint of panic or desperation, still comfortably in control.

Finally McKendrick steeled himself to do what needed doing. Circumstances had left him no choice. He glanced again at Horn. "I'm sorry."

"Not your fault," mumbled Horn, "not your problem. Do it."

"I can't let him hurt her."

"I know. Open the door."

With one long finger already on the button, still he hesitated. "Although . . ."

Horn waited, but nothing followed. Bizarrely, he found himself growing impatient. "Although *what?*"

McKendrick was regarding the monitor with one of those intelligent, speculative looks that Horn imagined was the last thing seen by any number of CEOs before they went on gardening leave. "Although," McKendrick repeated slowly, "actually he isn't hurting her, is he?"

"*Yet,*" said Horn, underlining heavily. "He isn't hurting her *yet.*"

"Quite." But other thoughts were marshaling behind his eyes. "I wonder why not."

"*What?*"

"Okay," said McKendrick quickly, "I could have put that better. But think about it. He knows we're watching these monitors—it's what they're for. He knows we know he's got Beth. Now, he might wait a minute while we wail and gnash our teeth a bit, but after that he's going to want to focus my attention. So why isn't he hurting her? Making her yell, and bleed? Why is he standing there as if he's got all the time in the world and doesn't mind how long I think about what to do next?"

"Because he has," suggested Hood grimly, "and he doesn't?"

"Nobody's that safe. And a real professional should know it. Anything could happen. Someone could spot our tablecloth and come to investigate. Beth might get away from him. I might make a last stand with Grampa's old elephant gun—anything. To make sure I do what he wants me to do, he needs to keep driving events forward, not give me time to look for options. He took Beth because he reckoned the moment I saw that I'd open the front door and kick you down the steps. So why does he not care that I haven't done it yet? Why isn't he using the one very obvious advantage he holds to force me?"

"Maybe he's giving you time to come to terms with what you have to do."

"He doesn't want me coming to terms with it," said McKendrick, shaking his head insistently. "He wants me acting on raw emotion. That way he knows what I'll do—what any father would do. It's not in his interests to give me time to think. He should be hurting her by now. He doesn't have to kill her. He doesn't want me to think he's killed her. He just wants me to know that he's prepared to hurt her, and he'll keep hurting her until I give in."

Nicky Horn had never known anyone like Robert McKendrick. Not even the man who'd paid someone to kill him. Tommy Hanratty was a thug, plain and simple, but when it came to coolheaded, coldhearted intellectual viciousness, the city gent took the biscuit every time. Horn's eyes were shocked. "Keep standing there," he managed thickly, "and he probably will."

Still McKendrick waited. "But I've *been* standing here, for a couple of minutes now. And I still haven't opened the door. So what he's got to reckon is that I've decided not to. That I'm calling his bluff. That I'm putting my integrity ahead of my daughter's safety."

"It's not a question of integrity," began Horn; but McKendrick hadn't finished, dismissed his interruption with a perfunctory movement of one hand and went on.

"A man like that must know a lot about human nature. He'll have been in this situation before. He must have come up against people who thought they could stand strong against the worst he could throw at them. And he knows they can't—that nobody can and nobody does. He knows they all fold the moment it becomes real. When it stops being a threat and becomes actual butchery. He knows I'm not going to hold to a principle once he starts chopping my daughter's fingers off.

"So why isn't he doing it?"

And when the question was put to him like that, Horn didn't know the answer either.

"Do you have a mobile phone?"

Horn's head was still reeling. He couldn't keep up with McKendrick's lightning forays into the heart of darkness. "Er—Beth has them."

McKendrick shook his head. "She has ours. Have *you* got one—in your rucksack, maybe?"

"There's no signal."

"Just answer the question. It's a very simple question, but it could be a matter of life and death. Specifically, yours. Do you have a mobile phone?"

"Yes. In my toolbag." McKendrick threw him the heavy canvas

bag as if it weighed nothing. Horn fumbled for the phone, turned it on. "See . . ."

But what they both saw was the signal indicator come up. Not strongly, but enough to make calls.

Horn didn't understand. "Why would mine work when yours wouldn't? Different network? Or maybe . . ." He couldn't think of an *or maybe*.

McKendrick could. He put his hand out and Horn gave him the phone. But he didn't use it. He put it in his pocket.

Horn stared at him as if he were mad. "We can get help now. Call the police. Tell them we need help!"

McKendrick gave a weary, disappointed sigh. "Nicky—there's a reason the man Tommy Hanratty hired to kill you, the professional who was chosen because he wouldn't let anything stop him carrying out the contract, isn't killing my daughter slowly while I watch. He isn't hurting her, and he isn't going to hurt her, because they're on the same side."

It had to be the shock, or maybe that combined with a little leftover concussion, because still Horn could make no sense of what McKendrick was saying. "You mean, they both hate my living guts?"

McKendrick breathed heavily at him. He really didn't want to put it into words. But he needed Horn to understand, so he was going to have to. Handy as the young man was halfway up a mountain, when it came to anything subtle or complex he was one chisel short of a tool kit. "I mean, they're both working for Tommy Hanratty."

CHAPTER 14

Nicky Horn honestly thought he'd misheard. "Sorry—weren't we talking about Beth?"

So McKendrick spelled it out for him—reluctantly, because once the words were said, they couldn't be recalled. He'd been hoping to widen their options. Instead he'd narrowed them. Now he could call the police, he couldn't afford to. Whatever else he did and didn't want, his first priority was what it had always been: to protect his daughter.

"That's how he found us. She phoned him. At least, she phoned Hanratty, and he called his mechanic." But euphemisms didn't work with Horn. "His hit man."

This time Horn understood what he was being told. But he thought McKendrick was wrong. He shook his head with conviction. "The phones weren't working, remember? There was no signal. You kept taking them onto the roof to look for one, but they were dead."

"There was never a problem with the signal," sighed McKendrick. "Beth had the phones. Beth kept taking them upstairs and saying she'd had no luck. She didn't want me to call for help. She wanted to give Hanratty's man time to arrive."

"But . . . he followed us. You said he followed us."

"He didn't."

"You can't know that. He's a pro—this stuff is second nature to him. He could follow you from here to Timbuktu and you'd never see him."

"It isn't the same man."

"No?" Horn looked at the monitor again, his head tilting to one side. He could only see part of the man's face behind Beth's head, but he thought perhaps McKendrick was right. "Okay, so there's two of them."

"No. Only one of them works for Tommy Hanratty. This one." McKendrick nodded at the screen. He hesitated only a moment before putting the rest of his cards on the table. "The other one— the one who broke into your flat—was working for me."

Anyone who does anything remotely dangerous, either as a living or for fun, knows that moment when everything changes. When the quarry turns and becomes the hunter; when the sea decides to swallow you; when the mountain has had enough and shrugs you off. If you've only ever read about it in books, you'd think that lightning reactions are what save you then. Snatch up the rifle, throw over the helm, slam in the ice ax. The truth is a little different. What usually saves you is freezing for the split second that prevents you from making a bad decision. It's more important not to do the wrong thing than it is to do the right thing.

Horn froze now. His muscles froze, locking his bones into a half crouch in front of the security screens. His expression froze, at the point that the tender green shoots of comprehension were pushing through the heavy clay of confusion. What remained active—what speeded up, in fact, fed by the electrical energy saved by temporarily closing down his body—was his mind. It raced. His eyes narrowed and darkened as the thoughts spun and connected and amassed information like the cogs of a Difference Engine.

So he didn't say, "What?" again. He didn't accuse McKendrick of making it up. He didn't even take a swing at him, although he might have done if his muscles had unfrozen a little quicker. Instead he said in a low voice, "You hired someone to beat me up?"

"Yes."

"You hired someone to break into my room while I was asleep, wave a gun at me and make me think I was going to die? *Why?*" But the answer was obvious. "So you could rescue me, and I'd owe you a favor."

"Exactly so." McKendrick didn't sound as if he was confessing to something wicked. "That's how I know he didn't follow us here. He took his money and went home to his girlfriend, who's called Stacey and has fifteen-month-old twin girls. He's a bit-part actor, although he works as a nightclub bouncer at weekends. He says he's going to marry Stacey and use the money as a deposit on a two-up two-down in Derby."

"You *paid* someone to beat me up!"

"Yes. Yes, I did. Get over it."

"I never did you any harm!"

"I know. I'd have offered you the money, but I didn't think it would achieve the same result."

Horn stared at him almost more in astonishment than anger. "You've got me killed! Between you, you and your crazy daughter, you've driven me out of a place where I was safe, at least for a while, and brought me here, and told the guy who wants me dead where to find me. I'm going to die here, not because I got tired and made a mistake but because you wanted the kind of help you can't advertise for in the *Tatler*! And all for nothing. I was never going to do what you wanted me to do. I was never the man you thought I was."

McKendrick gave a sullen sniff. "Whose fault is that? All this could have been avoided if you'd been honest about what happened up that mountain."

"I didn't want . . . ! I was trying . . . I didn't want to hurt any-one's feelings!"

McKendrick snorted. "You know what the road to hell's paved with, don't you?"

Horn shook his head in a kind of wonder. "That's your let-off, is it? Your get-out-of-jail-free card. I did something stupid. In the heat of a moment when I was shocked and, yes, embarrassed, I said things that hurt my friend, and one way or another—because he wanted to die, or because he wasn't concentrating on the climb and made a mistake—it cost him his life. And I lied to protect his reputation and his family's feelings. Maybe that *was* wrong. Maybe it was stupid. But it doesn't make you any less responsible for what's happened already and what's going to happen now.

"My life is going to end here." McKendrick heard Horn's voice shake, and it wasn't with fear or even anger so much as the sheer enormity of it. The recognition that McKendrick's plotting was go-ing to cost him everything. "Maybe it wasn't one of the great lives of all times. Maybe I didn't do anything very memorable with it—create a piece of great art, support a great cause, or just make a woman happy and raise a family. Maybe it was a life full of mistakes and regrets. But it was mine, the only one I was given. And you've thrown it away because you thought that one day you might need a dog—someone to come running when you whistled and jump through hoops in return for a biscuit. You killed me, Mr. McKendrick, as surely as if you'd cut my throat. And I didn't deserve that."

McKendrick felt the flush travel up his cheeks in a way he had not for years—decades, even. Not because it was that long since he'd last done something wrong, even very wrong, but because when you reach a certain level in the business world you acquire a kind of fireproofing. People don't tell you what they think. They tell you what they think you want to hear; or what they think someone else wants you to hear; or what it may be necessary for you to understand. They talk about profit-and-loss accounts, the best interests of the shareholders, the corporate decision-making process. Sometimes, while they're talking about the corporate decision-making process and the best interests of shareholders, they reach down and rip the rug clean out from under you. But they never look you in the eye and say that you've done something bad. Something wicked. The people who would do that, because they've suffered as a result of your desires and ambitions, are never allowed through the foyer.

McKendrick responded as a petulant child might have done—a spoiled child unused to having his actions questioned. "Don't be such a drama queen. We'll sort this out. *I'll* sort it out. Nobody's going to die today."

"*You'll* sort it out?" hooted Horn. "A man who uses other people as a fire wall between him and his own genetics is going to have a quiet word with another man who had only contempt for his son when he was alive and, when he was dead, sent a hit man after his best friend. And then everything will be all right, will it? Tommy Hanratty will send me a Sorry I Tried to Kill You card and a nice bottle of wine; his hit man will quietly pack up his arsenal and go home; and your crazy daughter will stop blaming me for the fact that Patrick wanted me in his bed and not her!"

McKendrick's voice was like gravel—cold, sharp and gray. "What you don't understand, Nicky, is that, finally, everything comes down to money. If it's going to take blood money to get you out of this, I'll pay it."

Nicky Horn was born a physical being. He was up on his feet and, yes, climbing long before anything recognizable as words were coming from his mouth. At school he excelled at sports, dragged his feet through everything else except woodwork. Even the job he did depended, to an unusual degree in these mechanized days, on the strength of his muscles and the skill of his hands.

In spite of that, he was never a violent man. Perhaps he'd always known that if you hit a man with a fist made of fingers that could, jammed into a crevice of rock, hold the entire weight of your swinging body, he was going to stay hit. A few years ago, before fear and exhaustion took their toll, he'd been quick to anger, too ready with a hot retort. But he'd never used his fists.

There's a first time for everything. He'd never have a better excuse; indeed, he might never have another opportunity. Maybe he wasn't firing on all cylinders, but he put everything he had behind his strong left arm and had the satisfaction of seeing Robert McKendrick stagger backward across his hall with an expression of utter amazement stamped on his face and blood spurting from his nose.

"You *arrogant* bloody man," he snarled while McKendrick sprawled on the floor, groping for a piece of furniture that would help him to rise or at least remind him which way was up. "You really think that everything can be bought, don't you? Everything can be paid for. Which makes you no better than Tommy Hanratty, or even any different. You both think you're entitled to anything you want, to use people any way that suits you. At least he's an honest thug—he doesn't pretend to be anything else. He never lied to me. He said he'd get me one way or another, and that's what he's done. He never pretended to be my friend. He never pretended that he wanted to help me."

Despairing of finding his handkerchief—of even finding his pockets while his head was swimming like this—McKendrick smeared the blood from his mouth with a sleeve. His voice was thick, with shock and contempt.

"Grow up, Nicky. Yes, I tricked you—but, God, you made it easy. Did you really think a total stranger would risk his own life to save you? Look at you—you're nothing. You weren't much before Patrick died, now you're an itinerant workman living just one step above the gutter. No one will even notice if you disappear. Hanratty won't have policemen beating down his door and reporters camped outside his gate. Fifteen years down the line someone making a documentary about death in the mountains might wonder what happened to you, but even he won't go to much trouble to find out. You're not important, not to anyone.

"I could have given you a better life than that. I still can. Sneer at my money if you want to, but be honest—the only people who claim money doesn't matter are those who haven't got any. I have a lot. I can use some of it buying your freedom. I can find someone Hanratty respects, or fears, or owes something to, and buy his help. I can pay off the contract and make sure Hanratty doesn't take out another one. I probably can't make him like you, but I can stop him killing you. With money.

"The deal is what it always was. I have money to spare, and you have time. You want to do a trade? But think carefully before you hit me again. I can find someone else to do what I need doing. And I don't think you can."

Horn went on staring hotly at him, but his fists stayed by his sides. He was used to being out of his depth. He hadn't touched bottom since that night on Anarchy Ridge. Even the sensation of going down for the third time was nothing new. But he hadn't known, until just now, how very differently the other half lived. Whatever McKendrick thought, it wasn't the money that separated his world from Horn's, it was the way those who lived there looked at things. Everything had a price, and nothing had much value.

Horn had wanted to believe—on a good day, *had* believed—that there were decent people out there, people who did things because they were right rather than merely expedient, and that if he could stay ahead of Hanratty's money, one day he'd find people who'd help him without asking what was in it for them. Because even the life of a traitor shouldn't be bartered on the open market.

Last night, in the alleyway, he thought he'd finally found one of them. But like Tommy Hanratty, like Hanratty's hit man, all along McKendrick had been looking at him with pound signs in his eyes. What he could be bought for, how dear he could be sold. When he realized that, something died in him. Hope.

He wasn't even afraid anymore, or only in the generic way that everyone is afraid of death. It was that close, that inevitable. "Mr. McKendrick, I don't think I can afford to have you doing me any more favors. Open the door and let's end this farce."

The older man recoiled as if Horn had spat in his face. "Don't be stupid. It isn't over. We know Beth's safe enough—she's Hanratty's informant. We have time to work out what to do next. Who to call. How to play this."

It seemed to Horn that finally he saw Robert McKendrick clearly. Not as a savior, not as a monster—as a trickster. He played Monopoly with real money and forgot that for the people on the board it wasn't a game. There was no get-out-of-jail-free card.

"Play it?" Horn echoed. "What do you think this is, a hand of poker? Amateur dramatics? No one else is playing at anything. Your daughter wasn't playing when she phoned Tommy Hanratty, and the man out there isn't playing now. This is for real. You've spent too much of your life in boardrooms, where arrogant, greedy men make the kind of mistakes that bring countries to their knees and still walk away with their pockets full. You should have been climbing mountains instead. You make a mistake on a mountain, you're probably going to die. It focuses the mind wonderfully. It stops you thinking that, if things go wrong, you can always cash in your chips and start again.

"Well, I did make mistakes on Anarchy Ridge. I got a lot of things wrong. One was, I should have died there. That was the place I should have ended—clean and cold, with a mountain for a gravestone. Whether or not it was an accident, Patrick's fall wasn't the worst thing that could have happened. Only we should both have died that day. There was nothing for either of us anywhere else.

"I begged him. Beth asked me that and I denied it, but she was right. I begged him to cut the rope. I tried to pull him up, and when I couldn't I begged him to cut himself loose. So I wouldn't have to. I didn't know then and I still don't know if I could have done it. Maybe Patrick knew. Maybe that's why he cut it. He wanted us to die together. But maybe he hadn't realized how much I wanted to live.

So much that any kind of a life, even the life of a coward, seemed worth having.

"But he was right and I was wrong. I've had four years that he didn't have, and there wasn't a day in all that time that was worth leaving him on the mountain for." Horn sucked in a deep breath and straightened up. "Now open the door. I can't turn the clock back, but maybe that doesn't matter. I don't suppose time has much meaning for the dead. Patrick was right, and he's going to get what he wanted."

Finally McKendrick was seeing Horn clearly too. Not a pawn but a human being: hurt, damaged, but still imbued with a kind of inalienable dignity. For the first time in years he felt ashamed of his behavior.

"Nicky, you don't know what Patrick wanted! You don't know what he did. All these suppositions, you've cobbled them together in the light of what happened and the guilt that you feel. But if he cared for you, why would he want you dead? And if he did, just fleetingly, just long enough to commit to one irrevocable action, he thought better of it. Even while he was hanging there. He cut the rope. That's all you need to know. He cut the rope. He didn't want you to die then, and he wouldn't want you to die now. He'd want you to keep fighting until you found a way off this mountain too.

"I can help you." There was an intensity in McKendrick's tone that suggested he really meant it. "I know I can put the deal together. This is what I do, remember? I manufacture deals involving people with diametrically opposed interests, and I do it so well they all go away thinking everyone round the table had to compromise except them. I can get Tommy Hanratty off your back. I'm not going to watch you throw your life away when I know that all I need is an hour with the phone and we'll all be safe. Go back in the kitchen. Let me do what I do best."

And Horn thought that finally McKendrick was being honest with him. Now that it was too late. "Beth . . ."

McKendrick shook his head. "Beth doesn't get a say in this. When it's all sorted, she and I are going to have a long discussion about what she's done. I don't know what came over her. I understand that she was hurt by Patrick's death, and again by finding you here, and some of the things you've said didn't exactly help. But to deliberately try to get someone killed . . . I don't know. Maybe she needs to talk to someone."

Horn wasn't even listening. He was staring at the screen. Shock emptied his voice. "You said he wouldn't hurt her . . ."

When McKendrick realized what Horn was saying, he spun back to the monitor.

The man in the courtyard had finally run out of patience.

CHAPTER 15

A T FIRST SHE DIDN'T STRUGGLE because she thought it was all part of the pantomime. She tried to look frightened—it wasn't difficult, surrendering herself to the hands of a man who killed for money would have made anyone nervous—and hoped her father would give in before she got a stiff neck. She wondered about squealing a little, or whimpering, but she was afraid of over-egging the cake. She always felt Mack didn't really know her well, but he knew her better than that. She wasn't a whimpering sort of girl. She was a knee-in-the-groin sort of girl. A climber. Maybe not in the same class as Patrick and Nicky Horn, but a climber nonetheless.

Which is how she came to be in the courtyard. Hanratty's man hadn't broken in and got her: she'd climbed down, from her room beside William's, above the lockdown. While McKendrick was in the hall she couldn't raise the shutters, but that wasn't a problem for someone who knew how to rappel and kept her old ropes coiled in a rucksack at the bottom of her wardrobe.

She could have waited. Like Horn, she believed that a professional would breach any security sooner or later. But she also believed, like McKendrick, that the longer the hit man could be kept at bay, the greater the chance of something happening to alter the balance of power. Her father was pinning his hopes on it. Beth wasn't willing to take the risk.

So she dropped herself easily down the side of the castle, bringing her rope after her. Later, she knew, Mack would want to know why. The best she could come up with right now was that she'd seen a chance to get past the waiting man and taken it, only to find herself trapped. Mack might wonder about her motives, but she was hoping he'd be so relieved when the siege ended without any harm coming to his family that he wouldn't inquire too deeply.

A quick confab with Hanratty's man out of sight of the remaining cameras, then they took their places in the courtyard and waited to be noticed. As she waited, Beth pictured the scene inside the hall. Mack would be watching the screen intently and racking his brains. But she was confident he wouldn't think of anything that would enable him to rescue her and keep Horn safe. She had only to stay calm, avoid doing anything stupid, and wait. Wait for the security shutters to rise and the front door to open.

Though Beth didn't expect her father to sue for peace as soon as he saw what had happened, Hanratty's man seemed to. He hissed in her ear, "What are they *doing* in there?" and she sighed and said, "Arguing, probably."

"About whether your life is worth more to him than Horn's?" The man was obviously shocked.

"About whether there's another way to handle this. Mack hates being beaten. He won't give in to threats until he's convinced himself there's no alternative. He was never going to fling the door wide as soon as he saw I was in trouble."

The man shook his head in a kind of wonder. "Other people's families . . . !" As if he considered himself a pillar of society except for the minor detail of being a hired killer.

"Give him time. He's arrogant, not stupid. When he sees he has no choice, he'll do what he has to."

They weren't exactly whispering, because there was no sound pickup on the security cameras. They were talking without moving their lips.

"In my business," the man said grimly, "time is a luxury. Scream."

Beth sniffed disdainfully. "I don't do—"

The first she knew he had a knife was when he drew it down her cheek, letting the blood out.

She still didn't scream. She hadn't been lying about that: screaming was not a McKendrick family trait. But she sucked in a gasp of sheer astonishment as she felt the skin part and the silky, cool caress of her own blood on her face. "Wha' . . . ?!!!"

"Sorry," said the man, apparently quite sincerely. "Needs must."

"You're working for me!"

"No, I'm not. I'm working for the man who pays my wages."

"Who wouldn't have known Horn was within a hundred miles of here if I hadn't told him!"

"I know. And I'm sure he's grateful. But the bottom line is, he's paying to get a job done and this is what I need to do to finish it." He drew another line in blood down her face.

Y ou said she was in on this!" Horn's voice vibrated with horror and accusation. His eyes were bottomless with guilt.

McKendrick didn't even look at him. "She is." His tone was short, clipped; as if he had more important things to do than explain it all to a carpenter. He still didn't dive for the door. "But she isn't in control of it. She thought she'd be calling the shots, but events have got away from her. She didn't allow for just how much Hanratty wants you dead."

Horn didn't give a toss for McKendrick's analysis, right or wrong. Horn didn't care that the girl on the monitor hated him enough to throw him to the wolves. The man behind her was holding her by her hair and drawing a third bloody tramline down her paper-white cheek.

Nicky Horn couldn't bear to be responsible for any more pain. He reached for the keypad. "Which button?"

McKendrick slapped his hand aside. "That door is the last line of defense. For all of us. We've seen his face and we know who hired him—how can he let any of us live now?"

"You can't let him *keep* doing that!"

"That's for show. It's for our benefit. He's hurting her, but he isn't doing her any real damage. Once he has you, it'll be a bullet in the brain for the rest of us too."

It wasn't that Horn thought McKendrick was wrong. In fact he thought he was right: it was what he'd believed all along. But it was no longer relevant. Though there was nothing he could do to prevent these people dying, their deaths wouldn't be on his conscience. But he could do something about the blood streaming in parallel lines down Beth McKendrick's face, and that meant he couldn't watch and not try. He began punching the keypad at random. "Which one? *Which one?*"

The security system had cost a fortune: the steel shutters in front of the kitchen door didn't rattle as they rose, they gave a soft hum like a sleepy bee. For ten seconds nothing else happened. The other shutters remained in lockdown. Then the door opened and Robert McKendrick stepped stiffly out onto the back steps. "Please . . . stop . . ."

The man was still holding Beth by her hair, her head bent back over his shoulder, the knife—such a modest little blade—in his other hand, doing nothing for the moment but only the intention away from resuming its work. He watched McKendrick hesitate down the steps, unsure how closely he should approach. The door remained open behind him but no one else appeared.

"Spread your arms."

McKendrick did as he was told. He was in his shirtsleeves and didn't appear to be carrying a weapon. Even if he was, Hanratty's man was among the best in the business—he didn't expect to be outgunned by a merchant banker.

"All right." Slowly, smoothly, the man put his knife hand behind him, and it reappeared cradling a gun. He let go of Beth's hair. She staggered a little, then straightened up and just stood there, eyes stretched, too shocked to move away. Her arms spread in an unconscious echo of her father's. She didn't dare touch her face.

The man's left hand disappeared for a moment, returned with a clean white handkerchief, which he pressed into her palm. "Sorry about that, miss. I'm sure Mr. Hanratty will make it up to you."

McKendrick's heart hit his diaphragm like a boxer's glove. Until that very moment there had been the possibility that he'd read it wrong. That Hanratty's instructions had precluded doing the safest thing, which was killing them all. But the man had named his employer in front of them. That wasn't something he'd ever do if he meant anyone who heard it to live. In fact they knew already; and the mechanic knew that Beth at least had known when she phoned Hanratty. Still, as a matter of principle, McKendrick was pretty sure it was a no-no in the *Paid Assassin's Handbook*.

"Where is he?"

McKendrick gestured jerkily toward the door. "In there. Looking . . ." He swallowed and tried again. "Looking for somewhere to hide."

The man smiled. He wasn't a lot younger than McKendrick— forty, maybe forty-five. Lean, fit, but not particularly big and not particularly powerful. Unremarkable. Nothing singled him out from a rush-hour crowd of accountants and estate agents and middle managers. And when he smiled it was almost possible to think he felt some kind of compassion. "That'll work. Well, you probably want to leave about now."

McKendrick had got close enough to put his long arms about his daughter's shoulders. He held her tight. "Do you mean that?"

The man nodded. "Of course. You'll want to get those cuts tended to. I don't think they'll leave a scar—at least, not much of one. Do you have your car keys?"

McKendrick nodded, still scarce believing what he was hearing.

"Go on then. By the time you get anywhere—by the time you call anyone and they get here—it'll all be over and I'll be gone. The best thing, from your point of view, would be to say you've no idea what it was all about."

McKendrick made no reply. He steered Beth ahead of him, under the courtyard archway and across the gravel drive toward his car.

Hanratty's man watched them go. He was also watching the kitchen door. His gun remained in a neutral position. Everything about his stance, at once relaxed and alert, suggested that the moment the weapon was needed, wherever it was needed, it would be there. But there was no sign that the McKendricks had refused his offer, so—still keeping one eye over his shoulder—he went up the kitchen steps into the house.

H e'd been looking for Nicky Horn for eight months. It wasn't the only commission he'd taken in those eight months, but it was the most important and also the only one he hadn't managed to complete yet. Of course, neither had the man before him. Though he had a good excuse: he'd been shot dead in Saudi Arabia by a princeling who'd bought himself even better help than the princeling who'd hired him.

So Horn had been something of a thorn in his side. He'd been close on a number of occasions—close enough to draw a bead once, only to have a high-sided vehicle pass between him and the bus where Horn had taken a window seat. By the time the vehicle had passed, Horn had disembarked and vanished into the rush-hour crowd.

The mechanic consoled himself with the knowledge that it wasn't lack of skill on his part. What kept Horn moving just slightly ahead of him was exactly that—his ability to keep moving. Movement is the best defense against an assassin. If he doesn't know where you're going to be, he can't lay an ambush—and ambush is much the best way to hit a mark. You don't follow him, you go to where he's going to be and you wait. What usually happens is that sooner or later the mark gets tired, or complacent, and stops moving. He falls back into a routine. He takes the risk of visiting his sister or turns up at his grandma's funeral. For a professional, one mistake is usually all it takes.

Horn had been both lucky, if you could call it that, and smart. He had no friends left after what happened on Anarchy Ridge, and he'd cut himself off from his family. He'd had a variety of jobs, but they were the kind of jobs it's easy to move on from and that's what he did, all the time. Hanratty's man had no great difficulty finding out where he'd been, even where he'd been quite recently. He was never able to anticipate where he'd show up next.

Until Tommy Hanratty called him on the special number and said where Horn was two hours ago. The mechanic had been an hour's drive away—it was mere luck that it wasn't farther—but that was all right because nothing had changed by the time he arrived. He knew this because he'd phoned Beth McKendrick before approaching the house.

So he knew that the girl was willing him to succeed, prepared to help him. It made it easy to set up the tableau under the courtyard camera, the one he'd left untouched for that purpose. Speaking without moving his lips, he'd told her how to stand, when to keep still, and when to squirm a little. He hadn't told her what he intended to do if the shutters remained resolutely down.

Now the shutters were up—at least, the ones that mattered were—and the door was open. The man went inside, closing it behind him. The enormous iron lock had a six-inch key in it. The man turned the key and pocketed it.

Despite what McKendrick had said, he half expected Horn to be waiting for him, in the hall or one of the adjacent rooms, too proud to hide. He was mistaken. On reflection, he decided, a man who'd played footsie with death among the snow-topped peaks of the world probably wouldn't await the inevitable in a club armchair, like an elderly aristocrat in the first-class bar on the *Titanic*.

What he'd do instead was climb. He'd be making for the roof.

Too proud to hide, too tired to run: all that was left was to fight. Horn didn't expect to win. Almost, he didn't care anymore. He had to do it for his own satisfaction, so that he'd know he'd tried and had gone on trying to the end. Somewhere in the back of his head he half heard the drone of generations of schoolmasters declaring, *It matters not whether you win or lose, but how you play the game.* But they weren't the sort of masters who taught at the local comprehensive where Horn was a pupil, and it wasn't the sort of sentiment that appealed to climbers. There's no such thing as coming a good second to a mountain.

He took the stairs. He didn't take them three at a time, which he would usually have done, but a certain amount of energy was seeping back into his body at the prospect of action. Adrenaline, of course, and you can only go so far on adrenaline. But sometimes you can go far enough.

He hesitated on the landing outside William's room; but the stairs kept climbing, up into the tower, and after a moment so did Horn. Instinct pushed him upward, told him that he had one possible advantage, only one, and to use it he had to take the fight into a realm where he was at ease in a way that most people weren't. The stone steps narrowed and the windows turned to lancets, and looking out he saw the tops of trees. The rest of the little castle was out of sight below him.

He'd been this way when they hung out the Tablecloth of Truce. The turret, Birkholmstead's equivalent of a lumber room, was the highest part of the castle, and a dead end. The only way down was the way up. In such circumstances, having outdistanced the hired killer below him was no particular comfort. Still Horn climbed, his mind racing, trying to remember what he'd seen up here, what there was that he could possibly use.

Hanratty's man paused on the first landing, looking over his left shoulder into the Great Hall. For a moment he didn't understand the rusty jumble in the middle of the floor. Then he smiled. God help them, they'd hoped to keep him at bay with castle wallpaper—with medieval weaponry hung up for display! They'd have done better arming themselves with the chef's knives from the kitchen. Even those wouldn't have delayed him long, but they'd have made more sense than three-meter pikes and jousting lances designed not, whatever Hollywood might think, for pushing an opponent off his horse but to break on impact.

Of course, these were the things Horn had left behind. The mechanic spared himself a moment to wonder what he'd thought worth taking—chain mail, a morning star he could barely lift, a double-fisted broadsword?—and chuckle. A man didn't get that many laughs in his line of work.

Though he was as certain as he could be that Horn would make for the roof, he took the time necessary to check that the threadbare wall-hangings weren't hiding more than a few damp spots. He trusted his judgment, but he never took any risks he didn't have to. He didn't want Horn creeping up behind him, or sneaking past him and finding his way downstairs. The result would be the same, but it would be tiresome having to round him up again.

No other rooms adjoined the Great Hall. The man returned to the stairs and climbed to the next landing where he found, and checked, a single large bedroom. A man's room: McKendrick's. Back to the stairs and up another level.

Here there were two rooms. He put his ear to the first door he came to, and though he heard nothing, he knew someone was behind it. He always knew. Whether there were microsounds that went straight into his subconscious, or a heat signature alerted some primitive part of his brain, or maybe that bowdlerized version of a scent organ that serves humanity as a nose was better honed in him and his kind and told him things that his fellow men would have missed entirely, he had no way of knowing. But he knew someone was behind the door.

He didn't touch the handle until he was ready to go in. When he was, eyes and gun acting in unison, his left hand turned the handle and threw the door wide in one swift, smooth yet unexpectedly violent movement, and in the same instant he was into the room and pointing his weapon at the head of man he found there.

CHAPTER 16

WILLIAM MCKENDRICK stared back at him, eyes white-ringed with a fear that might have been due to the gun whose muzzle he was peering into or to the chaos demons inside his head. A thin string of drool slid down his chin.

It takes a lot to surprise a professional killer. This one wouldn't have admitted to being surprised now, and no one watching him would have seen him stumble, either mentally or physically. But he felt inside himself how the gears slipped for a moment, how the bogie wheels momentarily jumped the rails. He'd been expecting a strong young man who was possibly just desperate enough to fight back, not an idiot in pajamas.

There's a riddle that goes: What can you sit on, write on, and sleep on? And the answer is, A chair, a table, and a bed. If Hanratty's man had had one second longer, he'd have remembered that some problems have more than one solution. That the presence of one man in a room does not imply the absence of another.

Horn gave him no time, not even that second. As soon as he was through the door Horn was moving too, from the shadow on the far side of the armoire, heading for the French windows and not about to be stopped by the man standing in his way.

He was shorter than Hanratty's mechanic, but he was younger and probably stronger, at least when he was match fit. He saw the man register the movement behind him a split second before Horn barreled into him, lowered shoulder into the small of his back, like a rugby player in the closing stages of a Nations Cup when he thinks the umpire's looking the other way. Momentum did the rest. Locked together, the gun somewhere in the scrum but neither of them sure where, they were actually off the floor when they hit the French window and it burst wide. A ball of arms and legs rolled across the little terrace and fetched up against the parapet.

Even when he was match fit, Horn couldn't have lifted a resisting man and thrown him over the hip-high parapet. What he could do—what he did—was wrap his strong arms round the man who had come to kill him and, while he was still working out how to shoot someone apparently grafted onto his spine, throw himself over.

Beth, still trying desperately to start the car, heard a sharp cry of fear and looked up. What she saw made no sense. She saw two bodies, more or less intertwined, spill over the wall of the little roof terrace outside her uncle William's room and fall. But they didn't fall far and, clutched tightly together, came to a jerking halt still twenty meters above her.

Beth continued to watch, mouth open, like a child at a magic show—as if she expected that gravity would at any moment get back from its coffee break and they'd come crashing down.

But they didn't, and as the astonished pounding of her heart lessened she could see why they didn't. Nicky Horn had a rope tied around his chest that vanished through a crenel of the parapet. And he was holding Tommy Hanratty's hired killer as if he would never, ever let go.

E xactly like everyone else's attic, the turret room had been filled with old toys and old suitcases, odd skis, the foam mattresses off a pair of bunk beds, a scattering of mousetraps—some of them occupied—cardboard boxes marked *This Way Up*, and folded sets of curtains no one could ever have considered tasteful.

And rope.

It wasn't good rope. It certainly wasn't climbing rope. It was old and dry and beardy, and Horn couldn't have guessed what it was used for when it was new, but he doubted anyone had ever trusted his life to it before. Currently it was tying shut the lid of an ancient steamer trunk. But it was synthetic so it was probably stronger than it looked, and there was a fair bit of it, and he had neither much time to think nor many options to consider. So he tore open the knots with a blend of practice and desperation, coiled it into a rough hank, and headed back down the stairs, frantically hoping to meet no one on the way up.

Time pressed unrelentingly; but some instinct of respect that would have made his mother proud caused him to hesitate just long enough to tap William's door before entering. William McKendrick was sitting up in his bed by the open window, a cardigan over his pajamas. His eyes didn't so much meet Horn's as wander near them; Horn couldn't judge if he understood enough to recognize that strange events were afoot or if they were entirely lost in the confusion that was his everyday life.

Horn mumbled, "Sorry about this," and shut the door quickly behind him.

The big armoire to the left of the door was perfect to conceal him from anyone coming in, but though it was heavy enough for his purposes it was too far from the window. If he was going to do this he had to get it right, and that meant having enough rope. The bed was in a better position, and though it might shift under the weight it wouldn't go far. But that meant trailing the rope across the carpet, and a man whose senses were as sharp as this one's wouldn't fail to notice. Horn took a corner of the bedspread and pulled it onto the floor, trailing it with casual artifice across the line of the rope. Now it just looked like sloppy housekeeping. It was the best he could do in the time available.

Which had now expired. Horn didn't hear Hanratty's man at the door, but he knew he was there. Horn's senses too were pretty well honed. He sucked in a breath and held it, and ducked behind the armoire where he couldn't see the door open.

Only one chance to get this right, only one time to do it, and that was now, with the man on a direct line between Horn and the window. He emerged from the shadow of the armoire like a greyhound from the slips, an explosion of muscular energy, and he was still accelerating when he hit the man's back.

There hadn't been time to check the window, to see if it was locked or unlocked, to leave it a little ajar. His plan would fail if it proved too strong and bounced them back in a heap on the rug.

But the weight of two men hitting it amidships flexed the frame just enough to spring the catch. The French window flew open, and they were still traveling at speed, now trailing a length of rope, a bedspread, and a *Whatever next?* look from William McKendrick.

It was only a little terrace, which was good. No space to dissipate the momentum, no time for Hanratty's man to regain control. They piled into the parapet together, Horn's arms already locked around the other man's chest, and struggled for a moment on the point of balance where, despite his best efforts, there seemed every chance Horn wouldn't be able to force their combined mass over the barrier. He only knew he'd succeeded when his view of the castle wall suddenly turned into a view of sky and the man in his arms let out a yell of terror.

For another interesting half second they dropped, locked together in free fall; and half a second isn't long, but it was long enough for Horn to wonder if the rope would withstand the jerk as they reached its end; and if it did, whether the bed leg it was attached to, the rest of the bed and its occupant would follow them off the terrace and into the courtyard below.

Then the rope snapped taut. There was nothing progressive about it: one moment Horn was weightless, the next his ribs were clamped in a vise as the bight he'd made tightened under the weight.

He'd somehow expected that, if he managed to get them over the parapet, the rope would hold him while the other fell to his death. But it didn't happen like that. He'd needed to lock on tight to carry the man over the wall, and maybe it was the years of training combined with the climber's instinct, but his arms refused to yield their grip. As if they honestly couldn't believe what his brain was telling them—to deliberately let someone fall.

So they hit the end of the rope like a mad dog hitting the end of its tether, with a yelp of terror in Horn's ears and a gasp of pain in his throat; and above them the bed banged against the bedroom wall, and the rope whined its distress and then it too, somehow, held. And they hung in midair, half a meter from the castle wall, turning slowly while the rope held Horn and Horn held Hanratty's assassin.

With the rope cramping his lungs it was several seconds before Nicky Horn could find the breath to speak, even in a rasp. "Drop the gun."

It took the other man several more seconds to reply, and though his voice was shaken to its foundations, his resolve held. "In another universe!"

Horn screwed his eyes tight shut, trying to block out the pain in his chest, the weight on his arms. "All that's keeping you alive is me. If you shoot me, what do you think's going to happen next? My brain's leaking out of my ear, but I'm going to keep on holding you? Drop the damn gun!"

"You'll let go of me!"

When Horn had planned this last desperate strategy, pounding up the tower steps with death's shadow on his heels, it was never his intention to try to save anyone but himself. The math stacked up only one way: to have any chance of walking away from this he needed Tommy Hanratty's hired gun dead, and he could only think of one way to achieve that. It made the massive gamble he was taking worthwhile; because although there was a good chance that the rope might break, or the bed might break, or while he was struggling to carry them over the parapet the man might gather his wits just quickly enough to shoot him, that was as nothing beside the certainty that if he didn't take the chance, he wouldn't live long enough to regret it. He didn't fool himself that killing this killer would stop Hanratty's sending another; but that would take time, and time was Horn's friend. Given a week's head start he could lose himself where even God would have trouble finding him.

And yes, that one would find him too, eventually. But Nicky Horn was a young man. Eventually seemed like a lifetime to him. So he'd laid his desperate plan with every intention of holding Hanratty's man just long enough for his own momentum to carry them both over the parapet, and then let go.

What he hadn't allowed for was how hard it is for an ordinary human being, given any choice at all, to kill someone. Even someone who'd earned it as thoroughly as this one had. Horn hung on to him because that's what you did, if you had a soul worth saving, even if you weren't a climber whose reactions and muscles and deepest instinct were trained for this moment. He wanted to let go. He needed to let go. And he couldn't.

But he wasn't going to tell the man in his arms that. "You draw this out much longer, I'll let go of you anyway. I can't hold you forever. That's kind of what we're doing here, isn't it? Patrick Hanratty was the best friend I ever had, and I couldn't save him. You think I'm going to try harder for you? I wouldn't crack a knuckle to save your life; I wouldn't break sweat. Do what I tell you, do it now, or I let go. You reckon you can shoot me in the time it takes you to hit the ground? Because you're sure as hell not going to do it afterwards."

Knowing better than to struggle, the man had become a dead weight in Horn's arms. His voice was muffled. "I don't want to die."

Horn gave a gusty little laugh. "Guess what—me neither! And I don't deserve to, and you do. We're on our own here, nobody's going to come and help. If we can't work this out, you are going to die.

I'm going to let go and gravity's going to spread you across three square meters of McKendrick's gravel. The only chance you have is to convince me you're no longer a threat to me. And you'd better start soon, because I've had a hard day and you're heavier than you look."

"All right! All right." The man held the gun out where Horn could see it. He let it go.

"And the knife."

"All right." It was awkward for him to reach it, inching cautiously so as not to weaken Horn's grip, but he managed and the knife followed the gun into space.

"Anything else?"

"No."

"You're sure?"

"I swear it! On—" He stopped abruptly.

"On your life is right," growled Horn. Somewhere in the shadowy depths of him he was almost enjoying this. "Next question. If I get you down safely, what are you going to do?"

The man knew what was expected of him. "Leave you alone," he muttered.

"Louder."

"Leave you alone! Give Hanratty his money back and tell him I can't do the job. Tell him to find someone else—if he can. We don't like taking on one another's failures."

"How very . . . civilized . . . of you," managed Horn. He asked himself whether he could believe a word this man said. Funnily enough, he thought he probably could. Anyway, the only choice he had was to believe him or not, and Horn couldn't hold him for much longer while he thought about it. He reached the only decision he could.

"Right. Now, you're going to do exactly what I tell you. You're going to do it the first time, and you're not going to ask why. Okay?"

"Yes."

"I need to park you so I can climb back. Then I'll haul you up."

"P-park . . . ?" Mostly what the man could see was sky and, a long way down, the ground, but as they turned slowly on the rope, sometimes he saw the castle wall. It looked sheer.

"About a meter beneath you there's a drip-molding—a stone ledge sticking out over the window of the room below us. I'm going to lower you so you can get your feet on it. Then we'll find you a handhold. It won't be much, but it won't need to be, just enough to stop you leaning back and falling off. Then I'll climb up and send the rope back down. All right?"

The man was looking, over his shoulder now, at the castle wall. "There *is* nothing to hold on to!"

Horn snorted at him with a fine disdain. "I've climbed rock walls as smooth as this, and I've done it fast and loose—without ropes, without pitons. I know what I'm talking about. There's always a handhold." It wasn't true, but he said it with enough authority that it sounded true.

And in fact, chance declined to make a liar of him. His expert eyes picked out an eroded corner of stone where the mortar had weathered. He was pretty sure that, armed with nothing more than the penknife that was still in his back pocket, he could excavate it deeply enough to provide a hold. All he'd have to do then was convince a grown man that he could support his own weight with the slim bones of his fingers.

Before that, though, Horn needed to change his grip, so that instead of hugging the man's chest he had him by the wrists. For an octopus this would have posed no problem. "Raise your left hand in front of you. Put your knuckles against your chest and crank your wrist outwards. Move it up till it's touching my arm. Good. Hold it like that. I'll tell you before I make my move."

But he didn't. Frightened people do stupid things: they cramp up, they start to struggle, they try to save themselves when they can't instead of trusting to someone who maybe can. The man in his arms was already as frightened as Horn wanted him. So when Horn was ready, he just sucked in the best breath he could force past the bight of rope, then sent his right hand diving for the man's left wrist.

Not being an octopus, this meant releasing the bear hug, trusting to the strength of his left arm alone to defer just long enough the moment at which gravity took over. It was a risky maneuver. If he'd been doing this with another climber—if he'd been doing it with Patrick—he'd have been confident of success. It was the sort of thing they used to do for fun. With a frightened man of unknown strengths and weaknesses, and he himself both out of practice and currently somewhat dog-eared, the outcome was less certain.

Still Horn didn't hesitate, for two good reasons and a bad one. If the gambit failed and the man fell, he himself would still be hanging safe. And delay would only increase the risk, as his strength waned and the man's fear grew. Finally, the wail of startled terror as the man felt his connection to the world waver and his body begin to slip gave Horn a surge of satisfaction. It was time to repay this man for some of the sleepless nights, the weary fleeing days.

But no sooner had his burden begun to slip than Horn had his strong right hand latched onto the man's wrist, so that while he went on falling—and wailing—the limit of his fall was prescribed by the length of his arm. By then Horn had his left hand free, and though the man floundered like a fish on a line, it only took a few seconds for Horn to capture his flailing right hand too. "Okay?" Horn said.

The man didn't trust himself to speak. He nodded. Even that was a falsehood; but his eyes, staring whitely up at Horn, acknowledged that he was in the hands of an expert. He trusted Horn to take care of him.

"The molding's right in front of you. Look down and you'll see it. Feel for it with your feet."

Horn knew when he'd found it from the easing of the weight on his arms and the pressure on his chest. They weren't there yet. But they were getting there.

"I need my right hand. I'm going to let go of your left wrist, and I want you to put your hand flat against the wall. Don't worry about locking on, just put your hand against the wall."

Feeling Horn release his grip, the man shuddered with fear. But his feet were firm on the drip-molding, and his right wrist was secure in Horn's left hand. He reached out quite tentatively at first, stroking the weathered stone. Then he pressed his hand flat against it, as if he thought that what let geckos scuttle up walls might work for him too.

With his free hand Horn felt for the crack he'd seen, began excavating it. He opened his penknife with his teeth and dug the strong, short blade again and again into the ancient mortar.

When the hole was as deep as the blade could reach, he stopped. "You're going to think this can't possibly hold you. But it will. Do you believe me?"

The man, who'd been able to see what Horn was doing better than Horn could, shook his head. No.

"Your feet will carry your weight. What this is for is to stop you barn-dooring—coming away from the wall. Dig three fingers as far in as they'll go, then bend the joints as much as you can. Bend them till it hurts. Have you done that?"

The man nodded. Yes.

"I've still got you—you're not going to fall. Now, without straightening your fingers, try to pull your hand out of the crack."

He did as he was told. "Ow."

"Exactly. As long as you don't straighten your fingers, you can't fall. Now I'm going to let go."

"No!"

But Horn wasn't asking permission. He kept his left hand close in case the man began to swing, but he didn't. Carefully Horn reached across his body and put the penknife into the man's right hand. Right here and now, he saw no problem with giving a weapon to a professional killer. "You saw what I did. Find another crack and open it up. Crimp your fingers the same way. All you have to do is not fall off for about three minutes. Can you do that?"

A whine. "I don't know . . ."

"Well, we're going to find out." Horn might have accepted the human obligation to save this man if he could, but he didn't have to be nice to him as well. "I can climb this rope but I doubt if you can, so don't try. When I tell you, take one hand out of the wall, wrap the rope round your chest, and knot it. Nothing fancy, just lots of knots—anything you can tie with one hand. I'll pull you up."

Shakily: "Can you do that?"

"Anybody's guess." Horn shrugged, though he was pretty sure

he could. No gale was blowing here, no cold was sapping his strength, and he could find something much better than snow to brace himself against. And they were only three meters below the parapet. If Patrick had been only three meters below Anarchy Ridge, the lives of both of them would have panned out quite differently.

Almost the hardest part was freeing his legs from the man's embrace without pushing him off the wall. Once he was clear, Horn went up the rope like an old horse climbing a hill—not quickly, not easily, but plugging away till he got there. A last effort and he rolled over the parapet onto the terrace.

For long moments he just lay there gasping, like a stranded fish. From the bed inside the open window William McKendrick was watching him with interest.

Time pressed, but Horn needed more rope. As soon as he could move, he untied it from the bed leg and belayed it round him. Finally he leaned over the parapet.

"I'm sending the rope back down. Don't grab for it—wait till you feel it against you. Then take one hand, wrap it round you twice and tie the end in as many knots as you can. It'll pull tight, but a cracked rib won't kill you."

At last the man asked what he hadn't dared ask before. "Why are you doing this?"

Horn was damned if he knew the answer. "I think, because I'm better than you are."

He'd thought that climbing the rope would be the hardest part. But this was: pulling up a man who was essentially a dead weight on a beardy old rope that hadn't been designed for the job when it was new. But climbers are good at ignoring pain. Bracing his feet against the parapet, Horn ignored the protests of his chafed hands and went on pulling, often just centimeters at a time, belaying the slack off around himself and counting a triumph every time the rope bit into his shoulder. Each bite was a bit more rope he wouldn't have to pull again, a bit more old rope no longer in danger of breaking.

Braced against the parapet he couldn't see the load he was hauling, could only imagine how long this felt to be taking to the man below. But he heard no complaints, nor did he expect to. This was hard on both of them; but only one of them had no alternative, and he knew when to keep his mouth shut.

All the same, Horn was beginning to wonder if something peculiar had happened to the rope—if it was slowly stretching under the weight so that, however long he pulled at it, he would never reach the man on the end. But then between one haul and the next, a hand appeared at a crenel of the parapet.

Which didn't mean the job was done. A last major effort was required of both of them. But it was the light at the end of the tunnel, and Nicky Horn spared himself a moment to catch his breath and look forward to a time without twelve stone on a thin rope digging into his shoulder.

The first he knew that they were not alone was when Robert McKendrick walked past him.

They say great minds think alike, and McKendrick had had the same thought as Hanratty's mechanic. He'd armed himself with a chef's knife from the kitchen. Now he bent and applied it where the rope came through the gap in the wall.

Horn let out a strangled yell but there was nothing he could do. The octopus could have held Hanratty's man with two of its arms and fought off McKendrick with the others, but all Horn could do was hold the rope tight, and shout breathless abuse, and watch with shock-dilated eyes as McKendrick's knife sawed at the rope.

All Horn's effort, all his climber's skill and strength that it had taken to get them to this point, went for nothing in the few seconds it took McKendrick to cut an old rope with a sharp knife. When it parted, Horn measured his length on the terrace and so never saw Hanratty's man fall; but he heard him. He heard the low, mournful wail as he fell, and the terrible, terribly final thump as he came to earth.

McKendrick looked over the parapet and nodded with every appearance of satisfaction. Then he put the knife down carefully on top of the wall, where no one could hurt himself with it.

CHAPTER 17

MCKENDRICK EXTENDED a hand to help him up. Horn shrank from it as if it still held the murder weapon. He went on staring at the older man with appalled, incredulous eyes while his skin crawled and his exhausted body shook. When he could get a word out, it was *"Why?"*

McKendrick shrugged negligently and took his hand back. "What do you mean, why? He was going to kill you. He meant to kill all of us."

"He wasn't going to kill anybody hanging on a rope twenty meters off the ground!"

"But you weren't going to leave him there, were you? He'd taken money to kill you. As soon as he was able to, he'd have tried again."

"No."

McKendrick grinned—humorless, a shark's grin. "Gave you his word, did he?"

"Yes."

"And you believed him."

"I was prepared to take the chance."

McKendrick turned away with a disparaging sniff. "Well, I wasn't."

"No one asked you to! He let you go. You could just have driven away."

"As a matter of fact, we couldn't. He'd fixed the car so it wouldn't start. Nicky, he never meant for any of us to get away. He was just splitting us up so he could deal with us one at a time."

Which put a slightly different complexion on things, even in Horn's raging heart. "That was . . . before . . ." he said uncertainly.

"Before? Before he cut my daughter's face to shreds? Before he followed you up here with a gun in his hand? Or do you mean, before you tied a bit of old rope round your middle and threw yourself off a castle wall because you couldn't see any other way that gave you even that much chance of surviving the day? Don't fool yourself, Nicky. It was him or us. It was always going to be him or us. It was better that it was him."

Horn, blinking, shook his head. As if there were stuff in there that he wanted to dislodge. As if there were a hope in the world that shaking his head would be enough to do it. It wasn't so much that a man had died. It wasn't even how he'd died. It was that the man who'd killed him hadn't so much as broken sweat over the decision. It might have been something he'd worked out at his desk, with the profit-and-loss accounts by his elbow. It was what made sense, what the situation required. And Robert McKendrick was, Horn had come to understand, a good choice for doing what a situation required, whether it was closing a factory or firing a CEO or cutting a man's rope when he was a hand's span from safety. Not a lot of sentimentality with McKendrick, not a lot of breast-beating. Just, do what's needed and move on.

Horn had thought he was a hard man until he got to know McKendrick.

Horn hauled himself to his feet—the hand wasn't offered again—and freed himself from the rope. He made himself look over the parapet.

And the mess on the gravel wasn't the most upsetting thing he saw. "Mack—what's she *doing*?"

McKendrick, aided by familiarity and spurred by fear, took the steps three at a time, reckless of a fall. Horn followed more slowly, but not much. By the time he reached the front hall McKendrick had got the door open and was reaching for the girl who knelt on the gravel.

"Beth. Beth! What are you doing? Come away . . ."

"He's hurt," she explained patiently. "He fell." She brushed off her father's hand and continued trying to sit Hanratty's man up against the wheel of the car. He was too heavy, and also too dead—it was like moving twelve stone of wet concrete in a sack. When she got his shoulders off the ground, his broken head tipped back, or forward, or sideways, and took the slack torso with it. Time and again the dead man hit the ground. Time and again, with the kind of bemused perseverance of someone who doesn't know quite what they're doing and so doesn't know how to stop, Beth leaned over him, as oblivious of his blood as she was her own, and tried to prop him up.

McKendrick turned to Horn with fear stretching his eyes. Horn had wondered what it would take to fracture his inhuman cool, and this was the answer. McKendrick's lips quivered and words babbled out. "She's . . . she's not well . . . tired . . . hurt . . . Help me. Help me get her inside. She needs . . . she needs . . . she needs to sit down. Beth! Come inside. She needs a doctor. Call the doctor! Can we? The phones were out—weren't they? I can't remember!"

"Okay," said Horn, as firmly as he could manage, "you've got to calm down right now. She's in shock, and so are you. Yes, the mobiles are working. Let's get you both inside, then I'll call the police and an ambulance."

"Shock," said McKendrick uncertainly, echoing Horn's words. He looked at him beseechingly. "Are you sure?"

Horn didn't follow. "You don't think she's entitled? With everything that's happened today? You don't have to approve of what she did to understand what made her do it. Her feet haven't touched the floor since you brought me here. She's been on an emotional roller coaster. Four years' worth of grief and anger made her do something appalling, something she must know in her heart was unforgivable. Then someone she thought was on her side took a knife to her face, and *then* she saw him fall from the roof and spill his brains right in front of her. Yeah, I'm pretty sure she's in shock."

"Just shock?"

Finally he realized what McKendrick was thinking, the specter that was haunting him. Comprehension hit Horn in the midriff like a mailed fist and his mouth went dry. "Of course," he said, though all the certainty was gone. "She needs taking care of. A good night's sleep, maybe a bit of sedation. Tomorrow she'll be fine."

"Yes," agreed McKendrick, and a tremor shook his voice. "Shock. Tomorrow she'll be fine. William and I have pretty much the same genes, but Beth's only got half of them. And she's only twenty-six. It can't—it couldn't . . . It's just shock."

He blinked and looked at Horn with a little more intelligence and a different kind of fear. "We can't call the police."

"We have to. We can't bury him among the rhododendrons!"

"What will we tell them?"

Horn shrugged. "The truth. That Tommy Hanratty hired him to kill me, that you tried to help me, that when it became a matter of survival we took him on. And won."

"I cut his rope."

"Yes. Well. A lot of people will think you did the right thing." The fact that it was true didn't make it any less ironic.

"How do we explain him being here? I won't tell them it was Beth!"

"We don't have to. He was a professional, it was his job to find me. He'd always managed it before, sooner or later. We don't know how. You understand? We don't know."

"What she did. Calling Hanratty. That wasn't . . . rational."

"From where she was standing, maybe it was," Horn argued weakly. "She'd hated me from a distance for years. Now she had the chance to hate me in person. And to do something about it."

They were heading up the front steps, the confused girl between them, talking over her head as if she were a child.

For a moment McKendrick said nothing more. He seemed to be considering that. "All right. Anyone might think it was fate sending them an early Christmas present. Anyone might think, momentarily, of taking the revenge they'd dreamed of. But normal people don't do it. They think about it, think how satisfying it would be, then reality intervenes and they don't do it. But Beth did."

They sat her down in the little room beside the kitchen and McKendrick sat beside her, gently cleaning her ravaged face with his handkerchief. Beth smiled at him and he smiled back; but he could see in her eyes that she couldn't quite remember how any of this had happened. Who had hurt her, and why, and what had become of him.

Horn went through into the kitchen and put the kettle on. Before he called anyone he needed some caffeine, and he doubted it would do the others much harm either. The spoons he dropped in the saucers rattled like castanets.

He put the tray on the low table and straightened up. "I can be away from here before the police arrive. You can tell them I cut the rope." He did the feral grin. "They won't need much convincing. Mention Anarchy Ridge to them and the whole thing will seem to make sense."

McKendrick appreciated the magnitude of what Horn was offering. "Won't they come looking for you?"

"Sure. But they won't look very hard, they won't find me, and they won't be surprised. They know about Hanratty's contract. They'll know the guy outside, at least by reputation. Even if they caught up with me, what would they charge me with? Self-defense isn't a crime. They'll go through the motions, then they'll move on to something more worthwhile."

"Where will you go?"

"I'm not telling you that!" Horn cranked out a thin smile. "I don't know yet. Somewhere I've no reason to go—that's always the best. Hanratty will look for someone else to take the contract, but there'll be no trail to pick up. It'll take him months to find me again."

"But he will?"

"Oh, yes. Eventually." There was an unbearable fragility to his smile. "Unless something happens first. Tommy Hanratty may have a change of heart. Slightly more likely, he may have a heart attack and his widow decide she has better uses for his money than paying a hit man. It's a head start. I'll settle for that."

McKendrick, his arm protective around his daughter's shoulder, regarded Horn for a long time before reaching a decision and nodding. "All right. Get on your way. Take his car—I'll tell the police I never saw it so I can't give them a description. And you're going to need money. I keep a few thousand in the safe—if you'll sit with Beth for a minute, I'll go and get it. Call me when that's gone and I'll send you some more."

Horn shook his head. "I don't want your money."

"You mightn't want it. You're going to need it."

"No more than I did last week, and I managed fine then. I can earn what I need, as long as I can stop running long enough. There's plenty of casual work around for a tradesman."

"Then . . . I won't see you again?" McKendrick was surprised by the regret in his own voice.

"Unless they pull me out of a ditch somewhere and slap my face on the front of your newspaper." Horn was making a joke, but both men knew it could happen exactly like that.

For some minutes they drank the coffee and said nothing more. Finally Horn went to go. But he paused in the doorway and looked back. "What will you do about . . . the other thing? You know I'm not going to do it, don't you?"

McKendrick nodded—carefully, Beth had gone to sleep on his shoulder. "I know that now. You were never a good choice. But then, you were never the man you were meant to be. The man you claimed to be."

"You understand why? Why all the lies?"

"Not really," said McKendrick honestly. "I can imagine doing what you did, I just can't imagine doing it for the reason you did it." He lapsed into a reflective silence as the echo of what he'd said caught up with him. Horn had embarked on the lie that was going to get him killed in a misguided effort to be kind. Kindness was the bit McKendrick couldn't get his head round.

He blinked and changed the subject. "I'll need to rethink everything now. What if it's not me who's going to get ill, who's going to need looking after? I can't opt out if Beth's going to need me."

Nicky Horn nodded, and stole a last troubled look at the damaged girl sleeping on her father's shoulder. Then he turned through the entrance hall and down the steps, past the dead man on the gravel, and out across the grass to where his car was parked under the hedge. Horn never broke his stride and never looked back, and he felt his burden lighten with every step.

Two years passed. Robert McKendrick made a point of reading those bits of the newspaper that didn't directly relate to business, but he never saw anything that suggested that Tommy Hanratty had caught up with Nicky Horn or that time had caught up with Hanratty.

Beth's face healed well. But McKendrick remained deeply anxious about her state of mind. He took her—protesting but resigned, humoring him—to see their doctor. Of course, McKendrick was less than candid about the reason for his concerns. He talked about the vagueness, the lapses of memory, the loss of focus that he'd witnessed in his daughter since the siege of Birkholmstead, and he reminded the GP of the family history hanging like Damocles's sword over all the McKendricks.

It wasn't enough—in truth, it was nowhere near enough—for a responsible GP to diagnose Alzheimer's dementia in a woman of twenty-six. He thought post-traumatic stress a much likelier explanation, and suggested that time and perhaps counseling would effect a cure. McKendrick demanded referral to a consultant; but she agreed with the GP. She saw nothing in Beth's manner or behavior—at least, the behavior she'd been told about—to justify even considering early-onset dementia.

McKendrick wouldn't be comforted. He knew in his bones that what he was seeing in his daughter was the start of what he'd already been through with his father, his mother and his brother. That the events at Birkholmstead were not the start of Beth's problems but a result of them. She'd tried to get someone killed. Four years after Patrick Hanratty died on Anarchy Ridge, she was still so consumed by hatred that she conspired with his father to accomplish the death of the man they held responsible. Any way you looked at it, that was not the act of a rational woman. To McKendrick, it was clear evidence that what should have been an imperforate barrier in her head—dividing the real from the unreal, memories from dreams, the world of experience from that of the imagination—had begun to leak, allowing the contents from either side to mix and meld.

In the end he did what, ten years earlier, he'd done about his brother: he stopped making medical appointments but trusted to his own ability to care for her by love and by instinct. For weeks at a time their lives were calm, pleasant and uneventful. Sometimes McKendrick experienced a momentary panic that she wasn't where he thought she was, but the gardens were extensive and McKendrick always caught up with her before Beth reached the hedge.

Once he found her standing in the courtyard, staring up at the little terrace outside William's window. Puzzled, she asked, "Who was it that fell?"

McKendrick said, "Someone we didn't know," and that seemed to satisfy her. They never again discussed what had happened.

Much later Beth complained, only half jokingly, that he kept her a prisoner in his castle like jealous fathers of old. McKendrick responded, entirely seriously, that he was trying to keep her safe.

She looked at him oddly. "I know what you think. That I'm losing my mind."

"No," he replied quickly, and part of him meant it. "But we have . . . history. We have to be careful."

"Has it ever occurred to you," she wondered quietly, "that maybe it's you? That what happened to Granddad and Uncle William is now happening to you? That when it comes to keeping us safe and secure, you've lost all sense of proportion? You keep me locked away in this ivory tower as if the world outside was a dark and dangerous place. But Mack, what you're afraid of isn't out there—it's in here, with us. It's part of us.

"Yes, we have a history. And maybe you're right to be afraid—maybe our history is also our future. But you can't keep it out with stone walls and steel shutters, and most people would consider it insane to try. If there's something wrong—with either of us—we need to face up to that and deal with it. And I'm willing to, and I don't think you are."

That night in the silent dark he mulled over what she'd said. He'd have liked to dismiss it as wrongheaded, perhaps symptomatic of her illness, but he couldn't entirely. Maybe she was right. Maybe what she did was bad rather than mad—an outrageous demonstration of hate-fueled rage but not in any clinical sense psychotic. If that was the case, what he thought of as caring for her was a punishment worse than any the law would have imposed. Imprisoned for conspiracy and attempted murder, at least she'd have had the prospect of release and the hope of making a normal life afterward. Locked up here, with him and William, normality was an impossible dream. If she wasn't sick now, inevitably his treatment of her would chip away at her personality until her illness became a self-fulfilling prophecy.

So he hoped to God he was right. And, even in the darkness and the silence, on balance he still believed that she was the one on whom the family curse was now descending. That she was the firework with the blue touch paper already lit, and if he lowered his guard for a moment something terrible would happen to her. Perhaps he had to believe it. But that didn't mean he was wrong.

The reality was, they were both standing on the frozen lake, wondering where the ice was thinnest, where the thaw would begin. And whether, when the summer was come, there would be any ice left anywhere.

And then, two years down the line, as he dutifully scanned the uninteresting bits of his newspaper, the name Hanratty leaped out at him.

The thing about glaciers is, they move. Everyone knows this;

and still, when things fall into glaciers and turn up years later and miles away, everyone seems surprised.

The glacier that had cut Anarchy Ridge into an overhang moved faster and traveled farther than most and, aided by a bit of global warming, reached the end of its travels in a little over six years. The ice cliff at its front broke down and melted on the banks of the Little Horse River, and one autumn morning a couple of hunters found the body of a young man in lime-green climbing gear lying on a gravel spit, his top-of-the-range boots still encased in ice. His knife was attached by its lanyard to his wrist, and all that was left of his rope was what was round him and half a meter more. It took no time at all to identify him as Patrick Hanratty.

A reporter braver than the others went to interview the deceased's father. Tommy Hanratty, massive and threatening even in a black-and-white photograph, stared unwinking into the camera and professed no surprise at all to learn that his son had cut his own rope to save the life of his climbing partner.

McKendrick made inquiries, but he never learned what happened to Nicky Horn after that. He never heard that he was finally living in peace and security somewhere. At the same time, and perhaps more significantly, he never heard that he'd died.